MORE THAN WORDS

Pink Bean Series - Book 9

HARPER BLISS

Copyright © 2018 by Harper Bliss
Cover picture © Depositphotos / belchonock
Cover design by Caroline Manchoulas
Published by Ladylit Publishing – a division of Q.P.S. Projects Limited - Hong Kong
ISBN-13 978-988-79123-5-4

To everyone who's lost someone.

Chapter One

KAT

"THIS IS the perfect location for a third Pink Bean," Kristin says, standing in front of the large shop window. "I can picture it already." She turns around to face Rocco and me and reaches out her hand. "And I'm very happy to be in business with both of you." I let Rocco shake her hand first.

Just as I'm about to touch my palm against Kristin's, my phone starts vibrating in the back pocket of my jeans. I sigh because I can so easily guess who it's going to be—Alana, trying to convince me, once again, to reconsider quitting The Lesbian Experience.

"This is a job perfectly suited for working part-time," she said yesterday, when I was silly enough to pick up. "Even one appointment per week would be good."

"Do you have to get that?" Kristin asks and quickly lets go of my hand.

"Let me check." I slip my phone out of my pocket. A picture of Liz appears on the screen. Relief washes over me and I pick up. Even though we used to be colleagues at the agency, I know she won't try to convince me to take another

1

client. She knows that once you're done with being an escort, you're done. That door has been closed once and for all.

"Hi Lizzie," I greet my friend. We've gotten much closer now that we're no longer co-workers—although we never actually, in the true sense of the word, collaborated.

"I'm in my old hood," Liz says. "I thought I'd drop in."

"Rocco and I are with Kristin at the venue for the new Pink Bean. Swing by here." I give her the address. When I hang up, Rocco's telling Kristin all about his interior design plans—again. His arm swoops through the air and his voice shines with enthusiasm. We've been talking about this for so long—although I'm not sure either one of us ever sincerely believed our dreams would come true. Then we met Kristin and everything started going really fast.

"Liz is stopping by," I say when a silence falls in their conversation.

Rocco checks his watch. "Auntie Hera should be here soon as well."

We make our way into the empty shop.

"If only we had a working coffee machine already," Kristin says, a smile on her face.

"My aunt will have the renovations done in no time. She's not one of those builders who say yes to a deadline only to push it back time and time again. I'm also her favorite nephew and she can't pull that shit with me." Rocco puts his hands on his hips.

"Family connections can work in your favor as well as against you," Kristin says.

Ever since we started talking to her about a possible third Pink Bean branch, she's been uttering words of advice like that. She doesn't talk a mile a minute, but she's been invaluable in helping us make our dream a reality. And as a silent partner she has invested enough money so that Rocco and I can devote all our energy to getting this off the ground as quickly as possible.

He waves her off. When they talk to each other, Rocco so flamboyant and Kristin so measured in her movements, the contrast always makes me smile. They're so different, yet they seem to hit it off. Then again, Rocco is the kind of person who hits it off with almost everyone he meets. He wags a finger at her.

Kristin peers at it as though it's a gesture not many people have ever had the balls to aim at her.

"Not when it comes to my aunt. Nu-uh," he says. "She's a woman of her word if ever there was one."

"A woman after my own heart then." Kristin gives him a small smile. I don't think she's capable of anything more generous, as though her genetics don't allow her wide grins.

"After we've talked with Hera, we can set an opening date," I say, my voice brimming with excitement.

When Jessica first introduced me to Kristin, I misjudged her as the kind of person who would take great offense at my then-profession. But looks can be deceiving—something I should know all about—and Kristin embraced the idea of the new coffee shop from the start. It helped that she already had a partnership going with two women who run a Pink Bean branch, slash feminist book shop, in Newtown.

"We'll see," Kristin says. "I know she's your aunt, Rocco, but it will also depend on the budget."

Rocco waves her off again. Kristin looks at his fluttering hand as though, if he waves it at her one more time, she might very well slap it away. "This is even better than mates' rates, Kristin. This is family."

Even I'm curious about meeting Rocco's aunt. I've known him for a long time, but I've never met her. However, I do know all about her long-term partner Samantha suddenly dying of a cerebral hemorrhage last year. Rocco may have cried about it when he was with me but I'm sure he was a rock for his aunt. He's that kind of guy. As camp as they come, yet with a heart of gold underneath. I love him to bits for both those elements of his personality.

A woman on a pale blue racing bicycle stops in front of the window, catching all of our attention. From her lanky form, I can tell it's Liz. She takes off her helmet and straps it to the handlebar of her bike. She waves at us through the window.

"I can't believe there's going to be a Pink Bean in bloody Bondi," she says as she steps inside. "Now that I no longer live here."

"Sorry, darling," Rocco says. "But this is where it's happening. You shouldn't have been such a lez and moved in with your girlfriend after two dates."

The three lesbians surrounding him protest loudly, telling him off for his inane utterance of clichés. While Liz admires the space, I see a bright red flatbed truck pull up outside. The driver manages to maneuver it into a tight spot, impressing me with their parking skills.

Rocco claps his hands together. "Hera's here."

We all watch Hera as she descends from the truck. She stands looking at the building for a split second, just long enough for me to take her in. She's tall with short cropped dark hair that is greying slightly at the temples. Her jeans are faded and marred with paint spots. The T-shirt she's wearing is loose and shapeless, but from its sleeves, a pair of bulky biceps protrude. Hera pushes her tortoiseshell glasses up her nose and heads inside.

Chapter Two

HERA

Rocco introduces me to Kristin, Liz, and Katherine. I've heard him talk about Katherine before. I know what she used to do for a living.

I've always had a soft spot for Rocco, as he's my only nephew, but I was still hesitant to take on this project. Especially when he told me he would be carrying out the 'interior design' of the coffee shop.

I glance around and conclude it's a good space. It's light and airy so it won't feel cramped.

"The counter will go here," Rocco says, not wasting any time. He's like an overexcited puppy. It makes me want to pet him to calm him down a little bit, but I'd better not embarrass him in front of his business associates. I know he and Katherine will be running the show, with Katherine putting in most of the money—apparently being a hooker allows you to save up quite a sum of cash.

Kristin will be lending her brand name and expertise, and is also investing a percentage of the money. What Rocco lacks in cash, he can sure make up for in sheer enthusiasm, I know that much. I'm secretly proud of him for doing this, for making his dream come true. Life can be so short, he's right to make the most of it.

"Rocco has drawn up some plans," Katherine says. "Which I'm sure he'll share with you."

I point at the backpack slung over my shoulders. "I've studied the plans already." I lock my gaze on Katherine's for an instant. Her eyes are dark and intense. I can see why a woman like her could hire out her… *services*. I quickly push the thought away. I'm here to help Rocco make his dream come true, not to judge his business associate. He's old enough to make his own decisions. I'm just the builder. I come in, do the work, and leave. "I'm here to get a feel for the place." I glance away from Katherine. "What you've planned for it shouldn't be a problem, from a builder's point of view." I have to admit that, though striking as she is, Katherine looks quite different than I pictured. She's much curvier than my idea of a high-class escort—but what do I know? She wears her curves well, however, and maybe that's where the secret lies.

And if I'm going to do this job, I really need to get over Rocco's friend's profession—or former profession, as he has assured me.

"You'd best not tell your mother who you're hanging out with," I told him when he first told me about Katherine's job. "She won't understand."

Rocco had shaken his head in that way he has, adding an exaggerated eye roll and hiss, and said, "Seems to me the one who doesn't understand is sitting right across from me."

When he offered me this job, I took it because I needed it. Not so much from a monetary point of view—although at the time Australia wouldn't let us legally marry, Samantha had made me the only beneficiary of her life insurance policy—but because I needed the distraction.

I need to work, need to do something with my hands to

chase the ever-growing cobwebs from my mind. If I have to work for an ex-prostitute, so be it. I've always considered myself an open-minded woman, but I have my limits. Trading sex for money is something that falls out of the boundaries of my comprehension.

"When can you start, Auntie?" Rocco asks. "And how long do you think it will take?"

Kristin steps forward. "We will also need a quote from you, Hera. On paper."

"Of course." I nod at her. I like her. She seems to know what she's doing, unlike Rocco who's been wagging his tail over this coffee shop for months now.

"You're opening up a coffee shop called the Pink Bean?" I asked him, incredulously, when he first told me. "You're not pulling my leg?"

He looked at me with his eyebrows all arched up. "Because we're all gay, hence the coffee beans are supposedly pink," he said, looking much more innocent than I knew him to be.

"Sure, dear," I said. "If that's what you want to believe."

I'm glad Rocco and Katherine have Kristin on their side for this venture. It makes me feel as though I won't be working on something that's bound to go bust in a few months' time.

"I'll get you the quote, on paper, by the end of the week," I say. "I can start as soon as all parties are agreed. I don't have any other jobs going at the moment." I don't explain why. I'm sure Rocco has told them all about how his aunt has become a sad, grieving widow. "The job is pretty straightforward." I give Rocco a quick pat on the biceps. "If we put all this vanity muscle to use, Rocco can be a great little helper if he wants to be. It should only take a few weeks. Let me have a proper think about it and I'll give you a better idea of the time I'll need when I send over the quote."

"Sounds great," Katherine says.

"This place is going to be amazing," the lanky, toned woman, whose name I've already forgotten, says.

"I'll do my best," I say.

Rocco puts his arm around me. "I know you will." He cocks his head. "When Chris and I redid our apartment, Hera tore down the walls as if it was nothing." He grins at me.

Katherine extends her hand. "I look forward to working with you."

I have no choice but to shake her hand. We stand around chatting for a few more minutes, after which I do another run of the place, inspecting its nooks and crannies.

By the time I'm back in my truck, already doing calculations for the quote in my head, I'm glad for this opportunity. It's time to get out of my house and start living in the real world again.

Chapter Three

KAT

I PROMISED Rocco I'd be at our future coffee shop for Hera's first day, not only so that we could both be present but also to mark the occasion that it is. But I also told him that I'm no good with my hands, which earned me quite the look from him.

"My skills have always lain elsewhere," I said to him.

"Of course, darling," he replied, throwing in a big fat wink.

Hera has arrived and she has barely given me the time of day so I just stand around, doing nothing. There are things to arrange, of course, but I'd reserved today to welcome Hera —and to help where I could.

She's pressing her fingertips against a wall, as though gauging its strength, but what do I know? For some reason, Rocco gets away with pretending he does know. She bends over and Rocco does the same. I find myself staring at their backsides. I already know Rocco's bum is pert and tight—he spends enough time in the gym doing squats, then telling me all about them. Hera's behind is but a tiny bulge in her jeans.

She has impressive arms, but the rest of her is lean in that sinewy, coiled way, probably from being a builder all her life.

She murmurs something to Rocco that I can't make out. When they straighten up, I ask, "Can I get you anything? Some water? Or coffee, perhaps?"

Hera points at the flask she brought in earlier. She does seem very self-sufficient. She doesn't respond verbally, which irks me a little.

"I'll have a coffee," Rocco says. "If only to give the competition some extra business before we seduce all their customers away."

"Have some of mine," Hera says. "I have plenty in my flask." Her voice is low but smooth.

"Thanks, but no thanks, Auntie." Rocco screws up his face. "I'll go for the real deal."

Hera just shakes her head.

"One flat white coming right up." I know Rocco's preferred hot beverage.

"Rocco, why don't you run along. Let me get a better feel for the place on my own without you two hovering about." Her tone's quite brusque, but Rocco doesn't seem to take offense. Maybe that's just Hera's way. Or maybe he's happy to get out of here already. He might have bulging biceps, but that doesn't make him the ideal builder's apprentice. They're, quite literally, just for show.

"Chris is coming by later," he says when we walk out. "He took the afternoon off."

"That's nice of him."

"It's not every day something like this happens in his partner's life."

I bump my shoulder into his. We're about the same height, something I've always teased him about, but today's not the day for that.

We walk in silence for a bit, until I say, "I get the feeling that Hera doesn't like me very much, even though we've only just met."

Rocco stays quiet.

"Or maybe it's more that she doesn't approve of me for some reason. Did you happen to tell your aunt what I used to do for a living?"

Rocco halts and turns to me. "I did. But it was a long time ago. Should I not have?"

I shake my head. "No, it's all right. I just get the impression she can't deal with it very well. Some people can't help but be judgmental about it."

"Ah, you know, she's old school. Religious upbringing and all that. There are some things she just doesn't understand."

"So I gathered." I start walking again, Rocco follows.

"You can't take it personally, Kat. She's had such a rough time. This is her first job since Sam died. She may be a bit rusty in the social skills department but her social skills are not why we hired her, anyway."

"It's fine. I don't need to be friends with the the builder." I sigh. "In fact, there's not much point in me being there at all while Hera's working. You can oversee things perfectly well on your own."

"Do you want me to talk to her?" Rocco asks.

"No, that's all right. Just let her get on with the job. The sooner it's done—"

"The sooner we're in business, K.Jo." Rocco almost shrieks.

"I know." As we approach the coffee shop we've been frequenting ever since we found the venue for our own, I stop in my tracks and look at it. It's much smaller than ours, but the front window is fully collapsible, opening up the space and bringing the outside in.

This place is closer to the beach and the pavement in front is much wider. Rocco and I wanted a window like this one, but, according to Kristin, it would be money wasted because of our location. She advised us to focus on coziness instead of trying to merge with the world outside and, instead, make it a place people want to retreat into, for a brief break from the real world.

"I still can't believe we're going to have our very own coffee shop," I muse.

"I know. It's quite the change, isn't it?"

We head inside and order our coffees. Rocco decides to give Hera all the time alone she needs and we take one of the tables by the open window.

"What's most baffling is that it's actually happening. That we're building something from nothing, from a silly idea we once came up with while under the influence of your way-too-strong mimosas." Rocco grins at me.

"As Kristin said, coffee is black gold and the gold rush is long from being over." I stare into my cup, remembering a long talk I had with Kristin about the almost inexplicable draw of a cup of coffee. How it can be so disappointing sometimes, when not well-made, and so intoxicatingly delicious when it is.

"You don't miss the old job too much?" Rocco inquires.

"I wouldn't say I miss it per se but it is strange not to be doing it anymore." I glance at him. "If it were up to Alana, I'd still be seeing at least one client a week."

"Good to know you're still sought after." Rocco sips from his flat white. "This is bloody good coffee." He looks behind him at the counter. "We need to figure out their blend so we can copy it."

I smile at him and, while we savor our coffee in silence, I think about my old job. I do miss it sometimes. But my decision has been made, and this is my new life now.

"Before I forget," Rocco says. "I promised Steve I'd teach

two spin classes the day after tomorrow. Can you be there for Hera?"

"You're the one who can't let go of your old profession," I joke.

"I miss the endorphins." He sits up straight and pats his belly. "And my six-pack is starting to disappear." He locks his gaze on me. "There's not going to be a problem between you and Hera, is there?"

I shake my head. After all, I'm used to people judging me by what I do—or did—for a living. "I'm sure she won't need me much anyway."

Chapter Four

HERA

"I'm sorry, Rocco," I say. "It's just something I have a problem with. It's a gut thing. I can't simply change how I feel about her."

"Just try to be courteous. Do your gallant butch routine. It can't be that hard to pretend."

"I believe I'm plenty courteous with Katherine." I do my best to say her name with a straight face. "Has she said anything?"

"No, but I've noticed how you are around her and it bugs me." Rocco knows he can be frank with me. After all, he has seen me at my lowest. "You're both lesbians, for crying out loud. If even the lesbians can't get along with each other, what's the world coming to?"

"Like you get along with every gay man." I glance at him over the rim of my glasses. I do love winding him up, although the fact that he has noticed my instant dislike of Katherine startles me. He's not usually one to pick up on things like that.

"Well no, but Kat's so lovely, if only you'll give her a chance."

"A chance at what?" I take a bite from my sandwich, while Rocco picks at his salad. I ponder his question further while I chew. I have no desire to befriend an ex-hooker. I don't say this out loud to my nephew, of course. For some reason, he's quite taken with this woman—and has been for a good long while.

"I'm just the builder," I repeat. "I don't have to become friends with everyone I work with. In fact, it's rather uncommon that I do."

"I'm just asking for courteousness, that's all." Rocco puts away the Tupperware box that held his salad. "You've been locked in your house for so long. I thought you might have forgotten how to be nice to other people."

"I go out," I say, noting that my tone sounds defensive.

"Uh-huh. Sure," Rocco says. "I'm not saying you should start dating, but good things can happen when you're nice to people."

My hackles go up. He's pushing it. "First of all, I won't be dating anyone anytime soon. You can interpret 'soon' as 'ever again' if you want." I expel a sigh. "And second, you can be friends with Katherine all you want, and not give a damn about her being a prostitute, but, to me, things like that say something about someone's personality and moral fiber and I'm perfectly entitled to not fawn over her for that reason."

Rocco holds up his hands. "All right. All right. Point taken." He tilts his head. "But you're going to be alone with her tomorrow, so please behave and don't act all superior."

"Have you ever known me to act superior to anyone?"

"You know what I mean."

I shake my head. "What I don't get is why any woman would choose a profession like that. Was she starving? She sure doesn't look like it."

"Let's not get into this any further. I won't pretend I can

change your mind about Kat, even though she's genuinely one of the loveliest, most kind-hearted people I know." Rocco glances at me. "It's just that… for someone who had to stand up to so much prejudice when she first came out, you can be really narrow-minded." Rocco's the one to shake his head now. "It's hard to understand."

"One has nothing to do with the other. Being gay is not a choice, we both know that. Whereas you deliberately have to make the choice to sell your body for money."

"It's just sex." Rocco throws up his hands in desperation. "Why are lesbians so bloody uptight about sex?"

"Your lesbian friend Katherine doesn't appear to be."

"Just… be nice to her, please. That's all I ask. I know you have it in you, Auntie." He bats his lashes at me, the way he used to do as a boy.

"I promise I'll try." I can't help but smile when he looks at me that way.

———

"Do you need me to stick around?" Katherine asks. It's the first time we're alone and she keeps pushing a strand of dark hair behind her ear.

"It appears I forgot my coffee flask this morning." Rocco's words echo in my mind and I'm doing my best to not see her as a hooker, but as any other woman—and my nephew's business partner. "Would it be terribly rude to ask you to get me a coffee from that place you always disappear to?" I throw in a smile and everything.

"No flask today," Kat says. "Whatever happened?"

"I had trouble falling asleep last night," I blurt out. "I snoozed through my alarm this morning and had to rush out the door."

"Are the renovations keeping you awake?" Kat makes

intense eye-contact when she speaks—probably a trick from her former life.

"No, nothing like that. I have bouts of insomnia. I'm not a very good sleeper on the best of nights."

"Hence the flask." She sends me a wide smile now.

"You figured me out." I find myself smiling back.

"A long black?" Katherine asks.

"Sorry?"

"Your beverage of choice? I've seen you drink your coffee black, so shall I bring you that?"

"Oh, right. Yes, that would be lovely." I shrug. "It's quite ironic that I'm renovating a future coffee shop and don't know the first thing about all the modern coffee drinks. I'm used to just drinking plain old coffee."

"Plain old coffee is the new hype. We'll have that on offer as well, if you were to swing by when this place is up and running."

I roll my eyes. "And pay five dollars for a cup."

Katherine gives a slight shake of the head. "The builder drinks for free, of course." She throws in another one of her smiles. I feel like she's working me. Is this how she used to break the ice with… what to call them? *Her clients?*

"That's very generous of you." I promised to be nice, but I just can't separate Katherine from what she used to do. I wish Rocco hadn't told me. I might have found her perfectly lovely if he hadn't.

"Anyway. A long black coming up." Katherine turns to leave and I only exhale once she's left the premises. There's an energy about her that unsettles me. I hope Rocco is able to free himself from his old job soon so he's the one I have to deal with while I'm working here, not Katherine.

Chapter Five

KAT

HERA STRIKES me as the kind of woman who hides her true self—her natural beauty—underneath a layer of dust and those wide, dark-colored T-shirts she's always wearing. Or maybe she just likes to be comfortable.

Before I walk back in, two disposable coffee cups in hand, I look at her through the window. She's mixing something in a large bucket. Maybe I should ask her about the building process as a way of having her open up to me a little more. But why bother? It's obvious she doesn't like me. I learned long ago to not be perturbed by that. Yet, with her, it's different. Because she's Rocco's aunt and, also, because she represents an important step in this new life I'm trying out.

When I walk inside, the radio is blasting an old Genesis song really loudly and Hera is swaying her hips while she stirs the contents of the bucket with a thick wooden stick. There's rhythm to her sway and she seems completely absorbed by the music.

I don't want to disturb her but I don't want her to have to drink a cold cup of coffee either. I clear my throat and she instantly goes back to her usual guarded ways. The sway of her hips instantly stops and she stands there stiffly, as though she'll never sway to any piece of music ever again.

"Coffee delivery." I walk up to her. She does have bags under her eyes. The rest of her skin is olive, while the area underneath her eyes is purple like a bruise.

"Ah, thanks." She takes the cup, then turns to lower the volume of the radio. "I could do with sitting down for a minute." She heads over to the corner where we've placed a couple of old chairs.

"Can I sit with you?" I ask.

"It's your place," she says matter-of-factly.

I follow and sit next to her, casting my gaze about. She and Rocco have taken down a wall and I can already imagine how it's going to look when it's finished.

"Not too bad for a drink with a silly name," Hera says.

"So, no need to worry next time you forget your flask."

"How much did that set you back?" she asks.

"Five bucks," I say. "Your estimate was bang on."

"I'll settle up with you later." She exhales a lungful of air.

"Don't worry about it. Consider it part of your payment." I gaze at her slouching shape in the chair. "You look like you need a nap more than a cup of coffee."

She pushes her glasses up and pinches the bridge of her nose. "As I said, I only got a few hours of shut-eye last night. And this is my first job in a while. It all takes some getting used to." She straightens her posture. "This won't affect my work, of course. No need to worry about that."

"I'm not worried. You're Rocco's family so I trust you implicitly."

Hera arches her eyebrows. "That's a bit naive, don't you think? I could be the worst builder and yet you'd still trust me just because I'm your friend's aunt?"

"But you're *not* the worst," I say, locking my gaze on hers. "And Rocco knows that."

She presses her lips together. "He didn't just hire me because he thinks I'm good at my job," she says. "I was also a bit of a charity case." Hera glances away, as though she has said too much.

"Rocco and I are pretty close. Well, very close, actually. I know your partner passed away unexpectedly."

"Hm," is all Hera says. "It's good to be out of the house. I reckon I only have a few more years of this job in me. I'm getting on." She chuckles. "Christ, I'm really not selling myself, am I?" She brings her gaze back to me. Something sparkles in it—something I haven't seen in her eyes before. "Please disregard this conversation and consider Hera Walker for all your future renovation work." She sends me her version of a winning smile—which almost does its job of winning me over.

I grin at her. For the first time, I feel as though Hera doesn't see me as Katherine the ex-escort, but just as the person she happens to be having coffee with. Something uncoils in my gut. "As a matter of fact, I've been wanting to redo my kitchen for ages. How are you with refitting kitchens?"

"As good as they come, of course." The smile hasn't been wiped off Hera's face. Maybe the long black I brought her is a couple of notches stronger than what she's used to drinking from her flask. She tips her head back and drains her cup. "Thanks for this. I feel as good as new." She jumps up. "Time to get back to it."

"Can I help you in any way?"

Hera gives me a once over. "Let's be honest," she says, "those manicured fingers were not made for helping me." She stares at my hands, which are wrapped around my coffee cup. "There's really no need for you to stick around at all. I'm going to plaster that wall over there and I can manage on my own perfectly."

"I'll leave you to it then."

Hera already has her back to me and she just raises a hand. It's as though the five minutes we just spent chatting, breaking some of that persistent ice between us, never even happened.

Chapter Six

HERA

I sink into Jill's sofa with a loud sigh. I considered cancelling, but decided against it at the last minute.

"That was quite the sigh," Jill says. "Tell me all about it."

"I'm knackered. I have this job going." I let my head fall back. "In fact, I could fall asleep right now." I snap my head back up. "But I pay you too much for that to happen."

"How's the job going?" Jill gazes at me with her pale blue eyes. When I first started seeing her, I never thought she'd look at me in such a confrontational manner. As though she wants to unearth the depths of my soul just by looking at me. Maybe she does.

"Fine. It's not too big but also not too small. The perfect kind of project to get back to it, really. And I'm working for Rocco, which makes it extra pleasant."

"That's good." Jill doesn't say anything else. She's definitely the kind of therapist who lets silences linger in the hopes she'll get me talking. I fall for it every time, even though I know what she's doing—she lets me think for myself. I *am* here to talk, of course, and at least, these days, I can do so without falling apart. I've gone through many a box of tissues in this office.

"Rocco's business partner's another kettle of fish, though," I blurt out. Most of the time, I don't even look at Jill when I'm talking, but fix my gaze on a painting behind her. It's abstract. Just a blob of colors really. Nothing I would ever consider art, not that I know much about it. Yet this very painting has now become a sort of solace. I've looked at it through oceans of tears and, like today, through hooded eyelids because I can barely keep them open.

Jill just nods.

"Her name's Katherine. They've been friends forever and Rocco told me long ago that she was a hooker. Although he prefers the term *escort*. 'She works for a lesbian escort agency that caters only to women.' That's how he put it. As if that made it more acceptable. As long as I never had to meet her, I didn't give it that much thought, but now I see this woman almost every day, I find her choice of career so… revolting."

"Interesting choice of word," Jill says.

"But it *is*." I throw my hands in the air. "At least to me it is. But I'm old, and Rocco says I'm way too uptight about sex."

This earns me a raised eyebrow from Jill. I've talked about sex with her before, about Sam and our sex life—it's one of the main reasons I first sought Jill's help. But this is the first time I've uttered the word in a good long while.

"Is that why being around her bugs you so much?" Jill asks. Before I found Jill, I had tried out a few other therapists, all of whom had a very monotone voice, as though any inflection could cause me psychological harm. Jill's voice, however, is full of life.

"How do you mean?" I ask.

"I think you know what I mean, Hera." Typical Jill. I've

been coming here for more than two years now. She probably knows me better than I know myself.

"Because she represents something I'm no longer interested in?" I almost scoff when I say it.

"For instance," Jill says.

I shake my head vehemently.

"You said it yourself." Jill doesn't shy away from painting the occasional smug smile on her face. I've always liked that she lets her personality shine through in our sessions, but right now, it bugs me as much as having to see Katherine nearly every day.

"Okay, I must have brought her up for a reason." I look at Jill with a hopeful glint in my eye. "What's your take on prostitution?"

"My take on it doesn't matter one bit." Jill told me this from the very beginning. *This is not a friendship, even though, inevitably, sometimes it will feel like one, but it's important that you're aware of the difference.* She tilts her head. "I can tell there's something going on with you, Hera. How about we try and figure out what that is instead of you asking me questions like that?"

"Fine." I know nothing about Jill's personal life, yet she knows all about my inner workings. It's a strange but comforting situation to walk into once a week, although it wasn't always that way. "I just can't be myself around her. She's a beautiful woman. I can see the appeal, but I just can't get over the fact that she... did those things in exchange for money."

"Would you like to name those 'things'?" Jill asks.

"Goodness, no." I jerk my head to the side.

"Okay. Then tell me what it's like to be back at work." I've been seeing Jill long enough to know she's not going to let me off the hook about Katherine this easily despite the change of subject matter.

"It's good, though exhausting. I feel I've grown ten years older since Sam died instead of the one since she's been gone. Everything I lift seems heavier. It's hardly a desk job, is it? But it is a satisfactory one. There's nothing like transforming a building, seeing it come to life again in front of my very eyes. I've missed that."

"If you haven't lifted anything heavy for that long, even the lightest load will feel like a ton. But you'll get used to it again, Hera. You keep on building." She cocks her head. "I can see the change in you so clearly."

"I have Rocco to thank for that. In fact, when I do the gratitude meditations you've advised me to do, it's mostly him I feel thankful toward."

"There's no one else?"

"Well, sure, there's Hilda. But it's different with her. Rocco just has this easy way about him. Even when I was at my most depressed, when I looked at him, with all his energy and bottomless zest for life, I had to acknowledge there would always be something else other than the despair I was feeling. He's just so… bubbly, even though I hate that word to describe a person." I shrug. "What does it mean to have a bubbly personality? I always thought it was the opposite of my own."

"And that would be?" Jill's lips quirk into a small smile.

"Cranky, and getting more so the older I get."

"You're not that cranky. Not all the time, anyway," Jill says. "You were grieving. There's a big difference."

"I guess." Something comes to me. "Maybe that's what I see in Katherine as well. That effortless bubbliness, or whatever you want to call it. That's probably why they get along so well, because they recognize that in each other, that same drive to always get the most out of life."

"Yet in Rocco you admire it and in Katherine it bugs you?"

"Well, yes, because Rocco's my nephew and she's… an escort."

"You didn't have to take that job if you knew it was going to annoy you so much to be around her."

"But I didn't know. It was only when I met her that I felt she was getting under my skin—in a bad way."

"You hadn't expected to react to her the way you did?"

"No. She's actually really nice. If I didn't know, I certainly wouldn't be able to tell just by looking at her. She's very… classy. Upmarket, I guess."

Jill nods. "And that offends you?"

"No." I shake my head for emphasis. "I don't know."

"Could it be that you actually like her, Hera? But you're annoyed with yourself because you can't allow yourself to do so because she's an escort."

"Actually she's no longer an escort," I blurt out. Why does it feel like I'm coming to Katherine's defense in the privacy of my therapist's office? Nothing of this makes any sense.

"Okay, my bad," Jill says, then goes silent again.

"At least it's good to feel something, even if only annoyance." I do look Jill in the eye now. "Remember when I first came here? I was such a mess. And then, with your help, I was starting to pull myself together, and then Sam died on me. Just when everything was looking up." I'm not saying this to garner Jill's pity—she made it very clear from the start that her pity would never be up for grabs—only to summarize. To make things clear, once again, in my head.

"As I said before, Hera, I can see the difference in you." Before I let my glance skitter away from Jill I consider that it might not be friendship we have between us, but it's something very meaningful nonetheless.

Chapter Seven

KAT

"Jess is running late," Liz says. On Kristin's suggestion, I'm spending some time at the other Pink Bean location in Newtown. Rocco's busy with Hera so I've asked Jess and Liz to meet me here. With getting the coffee shop up and running, I haven't seen enough of them—especially Jessica. I also want to get their take on the atmosphere. "She had an appointment with her surgeon and he's always late."

"Is she considering reconstructive surgery?" I ask.

Liz just shakes her head. Maybe she doesn't want to talk about it. She looks around. "What a cozy place." She narrows her eyes and peers into the book shop part of Pink Bean Two, as Kristin refers to it. "Look at that Caitlin James display over there." She paints a grin on her lips.

"Must be good for business." I let my glance wander around to look for any changes that have happened since my last visit. "We won't have a bookshop attached to our branch, but this is definitely the vibe I'm going for."

Liz quirks up her eyebrows. "Does Rocco agree with that?"

"Oh, we'll just dot some golden accessories around the

place—pineapples and bananas are all the rage these days—and he'll be happy." I smile at the memory of Rocco showing me a picture of a golden, half-peeled banana of which the fruit was also a lamp.

"How's it going with his aunt, the builder?"

I roll my eyes. "Let's just say I've been made aware that my presence at the site isn't required every single day."

"Ah, it's like that."

"Hera doesn't appear to be the most sex-positive of people."

"Rocco told her about you?" Liz asks.

I nod. "It's no big deal. And I know she's had a really rough time lately."

"That's no excuse for bad manners, Kat."

I wave her off. "It's fine. I mean, we might both have said goodbye to our old jobs, but it will always be a part of us. And there will always be people who can't deal with it. We've always known that." Liz and I quit the agency around the same time a few months ago.

"Hm." Liz sends me a conspiratorial smile. "How about I get us some coffees?"

"That would be lovely. I'm going to have a little browse in the book shop."

Liz heads to the counter. I venture into the book shop area of the Pink Bean. The woman behind the counter, who has her nose in a book, briefly looks up to give me a nod. She's wearing the same type of glasses that Hera does—the kind that seems much more suited to a bookshop than a building site.

I don't introduce myself just yet, although I guess that the woman must be Annie. Kristin has told me about her and her wife Jane Quinn, the lesbian romance writer. They were away when I first visited the Newtown Pink Bean, so I'm quite keen on meeting them today. But before I engage Annie in conversation, I want to walk around in silence for a bit, get a better feel for the place, and revel in what my own future will look like.

There's a display of Jane Quinn books and I'm drawn to them because of the connection they have to the very shop I'm in. I pick up one of the books and run my gaze over the back cover. I'm more of a non-fiction girl myself, but the premise sounds interesting.

Annie clears her throat. "Do let me know if I can help you with anything," she says. She has the calm and easy demeanor of someone who has been manning this book shop for decades.

I send her a smile. "Actually, I should introduce myself. I'm Katherine Jones."

"I thought you might be," Annie says. "Kristin said you would be stopping by today. It's lovely to meet you."

"Likewise." I walk toward the counter and offer her my hand. "Sorry for not introducing myself earlier. I just wanted to soak up the vibe before we started chatting."

Annie nods as if she completely understands. Then she fixes her gaze on the Jane Quinn book I'm still holding. "How about I call Jane to come down so we can all have a chat?" She looks at her watch. "She's still writing right now, so a little bit of patience might be required." Annie suddenly looks right past me.

"Is this Katherine?" a voice comes from behind me.

I turn and stare into the face of a very pleasant-looking woman, who also, unmistakably, makes my gaydar ping. I seem to have ended up in lesbian coffee slash book shop heaven.

"Mia Miller," the younger woman says. "I work with Kristin."

"Ah yes, of course." I've heard all about Mia. Kristin

never told me she was such a fox, however—Kristin isn't really one to indulge in frivolities like that.

———

Fifteen minutes later Jess has arrived and, instead of having a quiet conversation with my two friends, we're joined by Mia and Annie, with Annie promising that Jane will be there soon as well.

"Don't be alarmed," Mia says, "this time of day is always a little quiet, but it's the welcome kind of quiet between the morning and lunchtime rush." She paints on a wide smile and brushes her hair from her forehead with a gesture so assured, it makes something flutter in my stomach. Maybe I should invite Mia for a one-on-one conversation, as Kristin has suggested a few times already. I'm sure she can impart more than a few nuggets of wisdom pertaining to running a successful coffee shop.

"This gives us the time to chat," Annie says, as she adjusts her glasses on the bridge of her nose. She bears an uncanny resemblance to one of my favorite clients who went by the name of Mrs. Robinson. And I think that maybe I'm the one who has trouble flicking the switch, who finds it a hard transition from the life I used to live—the life that only a very few truly understood—to this atmosphere of utter normalcy I currently find myself standing in. Maybe that's what Hera has been picking up on—and reacting to with overt hostility.

Mia plays with a ring on her finger, a gesture I know well. I've seen dozens of women touch their wedding rings like that, as a means to ground themselves after they've been with me, to ready themselves to step back into the real world. It would be a small miracle if a woman like Mia wasn't involved with someone.

"When's the opening planned?" Mia asks.

"In a few weeks. The building's being renovated as we speak and the builder doesn't appear to be a flake." I throw in a smile. "We should be up and running soon."

"Kristin's building herself quite the empire," Jessica says.

"And yet she's always wanting to scale back her hours." Mia rolls her eyes. "Which she always does, only to start a new venture not long after."

"She's only a silent partner," I say. "But her advice has been invaluable." It was Kristin who got the ball rolling for Rocco and me and if it hadn't been for meeting her at the opening of Liz and Jess's gallery, we wouldn't be where we are now—a few weeks away from opening.

"Are you hiring staff from the get-go or planning to do everything yourself?" Mia asks. "It's you and another person, isn't it?"

"Yes," I nod. "My best friend Rocco and me. It'll just be us for starters."

Mia nods. "My advice—don't wait too long to hire people to help. I understand the urge to save on wages, but service and self-care are key." She tilts her head. "What industry were you in before?"

Jess instantly shuffles in her seat.

I find Liz's eyes and revel in the complicity in her gaze. We have a line for this—a different one for different occasions. Annie and Mia are people we'll run into again so I give them the version best-suited for that category.

"I was a travel agent," I say. "Taking care of people's every need."

Mia nods again. She seems to be taking this very seriously. "That's good. You're used to dealing with people."

"Oh yes." She has no idea.

When I started at the escort agency, Alana's first words of advice to me were to never openly tell strangers what I do, to always resist the urge because it's not about my sense of self or how empowered I might feel—it's about the others and how society has forced upon them the notion that paying for sex is always, unequivocally, wrong. "It's not how you want to start off a relationship, darling," Alana would say. "Any kind of relationship."

A group of women arrives in the shop and Annie gets up to help the ones drifting to the book shop, while Mia keeps an eye on the coffee shop counter. When the line grows too long, she excuses herself to help the person making and serving the drinks. I observe them for a few minutes, working in tandem, in quiet understanding, and wonder if Rocco and I can ever become a well-oiled machine like that. For starters, we will never be able to work together in silence, because Rocco can't keep his mouth shut for two consecutive seconds.

"They're lovely," Jess says gesturing towards Mia and her colleague, pulling me from my daydreams in which I picture my near future.

I look my friend in the eye. "How was your appointment?"

"Pointless," she says with a smirk. "You know surgeons. Always trying to sell you some more surgery."

"Reconstruction?" I ask.

She nods. "Liz says she doesn't mind bestowing all her attention on just my left breast."

Liz smiles at Jess and I'm so happy they've found each other. I resigned myself a long time ago to a life of single-hood, so much so that I've pretty much closed myself off to the possibility of the kind of love they share. But, now that I'm an ex-call girl, that primal urge to bond has been rearing its head once more.

Chapter Eight

HERA

I⊤'s the last day of the Pink Bean renovations and I had forgotten all about final-day melancholy. This was a pretty quick, not very invasive job. Nevertheless, now that the work is almost done, and I have the satisfaction of casting my glance over the results of my hard graft, I'm overcome with a sense of sadness.

It was pleasant to work alongside Rocco. Although the boy doesn't have any natural aptitude for this kind of work, his enthusiasm for his and Katherine's coffee shop made him execute the tasks I set for him with unseen zeal. His partner Chris often dropped by and helped out as well and I've grown fond of the companionship that has developed between the three of us. It feels good to live my life among real people again, instead of rehashing old memories of people who are no longer here.

I've barely seen Katherine the past few days, which has helped with my mood. She might be a sight for sore eyes but, as long as I didn't see her, I didn't have to confront my ambivalence toward her. I do prefer it that way, in this transitional part of my life where I'm trying to be less of a hermit and more of everything I used to be.

But, today, probably because it's the last day, Katherine's here. She isn't dressed for a building site. To me—and really, what do I know?—she looks more like she's ready for an appointment with a client.

I've been going over the conversation I had with Jill about Katherine in my head for days now. When plastering walls, the mind tends to wander.

I've concluded that my gut reaction was the right one—it usually is. She may look all dolled up today, red lipstick and matching nails, and smell like a million bucks, there's still something unseemly about her. Something I can't get over.

Rocco can have a go at me about it for as long as he likes, and Jill can question my motives all she wants, but, at the end of the day, I believe I'm entitled to how I feel about Katherine. And I'd rather keep my distance than have another conversation with that woman.

"You've done a wonderful job, Hera," Katherine says. She has walked up to me and stands so close her perfume wafts up into my nose.

"Thanks. It's what I do, so." I run a hand through my hair. It's getting too long. I make a mental note to get out my clippers tonight after I've showered. After this job is totally done. And I have to start thinking about the next one.

"I was serious about you having a look at my kitchen." Katherine looks me straight in the eye and smiles at me a little too broadly. "Can I call you some time?"

"Sure. Rocco has my number." I'm pretty sure I won't be picking up the phone.

She tilts her head and sends me a funny look. Is it a flirty one? I've no idea. I haven't flirted with a woman in years. Any desire for that died along with Sam. And I certainly have no desire to be buttered up by some professional flirting from the likes of Katherine.

"You'll come to the opening, won't you?"

"Rocco wouldn't speak to me for weeks if I failed to show up."

"He adores you," Katherine says, and something about it, maybe the way she says it, jars me to the point that I feel my limbs stiffen.

I shrug, hoping to end this conversation, this inane chit-chat. Before Katherine has the chance to open her mouth again, I point at the ceiling. "I have a couple of holes to fill up there before the painter can get to work."

"Of course."

I get back to it, positioning the ladder, and putting the tools I need within reach, but Katherine doesn't move. I feel her stare on me.

Before I climb the ladder I try to give her a look which I hope conveys that I don't appreciate being watched like that.

"I do admire a strong woman," she says, and smiles with lips that are too red for this place. All the walls are still bright white, there's dust everywhere, and I'm dressed in jeans and a T-shirt with a couple of holes running down the side, yet here Katherine stands, all smiles, in impossibly glam attire, with her red lips and red fingernails. She doesn't fit in here or, at the very least, her presence irks me. But I can hardly ask her to leave.

I start climbing the ladder but, for some reason, it sways and I lose my balance for a second. I'm only two rungs up and I try to regain my footing, but it's hard to refocus when you have two dark eyes boring into you like that.

"Damn it," I mutter under my breath as I, very inelegantly, jump off the ladder and have to take a step back to stabilize myself. I look down and notice a piece of cardboard under one of the legs of the ladder.

"Are you all right?" Katherine has the audacity to grab me by the arm. I shrug her hand off me immediately.

"If you could just leave me to finish my work in peace," I snap.

"Sure." She withdraws her hand while our gazes meet. Hers is soft and caring. Mine, I hope, is thunderous and menacing. I want her as far away from me as possible.

I kick away the unbalancing scrap of cardboard and reposition the ladder, using all my concentration this time, not allowing Katherine-the-ex-call girl to mess up my focus, cursing myself inwardly because it's stupid little mistakes like not properly securing a ladder that cause the most accidents in my line of work.

Before I attempt to climb up again, I make sure Katherine is far enough away. She's walking away from the ladder, her back to me, her hips swaying like she's on a bloody catwalk instead of a building site. The airs and graces of this woman. And what kind of clientele will she attract to this place? This coffee shop that has been my nephew's dream for so long. I do hope word doesn't get out about her previous job. Although, truth be told, Rocco's friends would probably be drawn to her for that very reason. They probably all know and coo around her as though she's the Queen of Sheba, while all she is... I halt my train of thought. Getting worked up while ascending a ladder is never a good idea. I take a deep breath and focus on the holes that need filling.

Chapter Nine

KAT

"ONE MORE WEEK," I say.

Rocco stands facing me and claps his hands together. "I know, *K.Jo*, can you believe it?"

We've been counting down the days forever, or so it seems, yet it still feels good. And it only gets better as the number of days decreases.

Rocco gives a big, exaggerated sigh. "The painters will be out in two days and then, *finally*, I can work my magic." He jumps up and down, which is always a funny sight because he's such a short muscle queen. He bulges his right biceps. "And with all the stuff Auntie Hera made me carry, I think I've grown some extra muscle to put into it." He turns to watch Hera, who's standing on top of the ladder she nearly fell from earlier.

Both her arms are up, one against the ceiling to steady herself, the other applying some sort of putty to smooth out the last dents. Her T-shirt has ridden up and I can make out the skin of her belly.

"Your aunt really doesn't like me, does she? I thought I

could charm my way into her good graces, but I get the feeling it hasn't worked."

"I bet that doesn't happen to you a lot." Rocco bumps his hip into mine lightly. "That you can't charm someone into liking you." He flutters his lashes at me. "This place will be teeming with lesbians wanting to bask in some of your irresistible K.Jo charm, girl. For that alone, this coffee shop will be a gold mine."

I chuckle. "As long as they don't know about my previous career. That has a tendency to turn people against me." I nod at Hera. "I've asked her to remodel my kitchen, by the way."

"Ooh, someone's not ready to throw in the towel just yet." He winks at me. "Is it really so important to you that my aunt likes you?"

I shake my head. "My kitchen just really needs a do-over and you know how hard it is to find a builder you can trust. I've seen Hera at work. She's thorough, fast, and reliable. She may not like me, but I'm convinced she'll do a good job regardless. That's all."

Rocco nods. "As long as you don't get any romantic ideas in your head about her. That ship has sailed for Auntie Hera and not even a woman of your quality and grace could ever change her mind about that."

I huff out some air. "Romantic? Are you crazy?" My turn to slam my hip against his. "The woman practically has to force herself to say hello to me."

"Just saying," Rocco says, in that nonchalant way of his. He probably didn't mean anything by it. He's the kind to blurt out silly things like that.

I look over at Hera again. She has descended from the ladder and is casting her gaze about the place. I can't fault her work ethic. She worked long days and has delivered on time. As far as I can tell, her job's done, and it's only mid-day.

"I think Hera's finished."

"Yay." Rocco does a simultaneous hand-clap and jump. "Can it be true, Auntie?" he yells. "Have you finished?"

"Just a few bits and bobs," Hera says in her usual low growl.

"Shall we take her to lunch to celebrate?" Rocco asks.

"You take your aunt to lunch. I get the feeling she wouldn't enjoy her meal all that much if she had to share a table with me."

"Oh, come on, Kat, be the bigger person," he pleads. "Do it for me, your best friend and business partner. I want to have lunch with my two favorite girls."

"Your mother wouldn't be very pleased if she heard that," I reply.

"My mother didn't just renovate our coffee shop in record time. She's probably at home filing her nails."

"Ask Hera if she wants me to come. If she does, I will. If she doesn't, you'll have to respect her decision."

"Will do, darling." Rocco shimmies over to Hera, who has started gathering her tools.

I watch them as he whispers to her. Hera glances at me and I give her a smile, because why not try to get her to thaw a little more? Rocco's probably emotionally blackmailing her and, hard as nails she may be with me, it's so obvious she has a massive soft spot for him—and can't say no to him.

Rocco turns to me and gives me a thumbs-up. I'm not sure whether I should be delighted that he was able to make a tiny bit of an inroad on my behalf, or deflated at the prospect of having Hera stare at me with nothing but contempt for the duration of a meal. Although, I could really have sworn that contempt's not all I've spotted in her gaze.

I think things are far more complicated than that.

Chapter Ten

HERA

I'M NOT SURE HOW, or why, I find myself having lunch with Katherine. Ah yes, my darling nephew. From the moment my sister Hilda had suspicions her son might be gay, she urged me to spend time with him. Hence, Rocco and I have been growing closer since he was ten years old and Hilda found him strutting around the house in her high heels with her lipstick plastered clumsily onto his lips.

I was the one to assure him that there was absolutely nothing wrong with him and that he was no less a person than anyone else. Conversations like that tend to create a bond.

Once again, I found myself unable to say no to him. So here I am. Rocco's sitting across from me and Katherine's seated next to him. Even though Rocco's been helping me apply the final touches to the coffee shop, and loading all my dusty gear into my truck, he still looks as though he's fresh from the shower. Foreseeing as he is, he always has a freshly ironed T-shirt in his car. I guess when you have the conviction to iron your T-shirts, it's only a small step to always having a spare at hand.

Rocco and I have gone for meals dressed the way we are countless times, but it has never made me feel out of sorts. That's who he is and this, faded jeans and spotty well-worn T-shirt, is who I am.

It's Katherine's presence that is unsettling me again. While we peer at the menu, I decide my best bet to make it through this lunch is to opt for silence.

"This occasion calls for a good bottle of wine," Rocco exclaims. "K.Jo, you do the honors and choose." He looks up at me. "She has exquisite taste."

"I bet she does," I say, before I can even stop myself. I can't stop the corners of my mouth from drawing down either. Being near this woman puts my teeth on edge. Thank goodness it's Wednesday and I have a session with Jill later today. Although I may not mention Katherine at all. The job's done. It's time to put her out of my mind once and for all.

Katherine glares at me over the menu she's holding. She doesn't say anything, just gives me a look I quickly turn away from.

A waiter comes around and we place our order. Katherine orders a New Zealand pinot gris. I sneaked a peek at the wine list myself, even though my opinion wasn't called for, and I probably would have picked that one as well.

Rocco, an expert at keeping conversations going if ever there was one, has barely had time to open his mouth when the wine is delivered to our table.

Katherine only makes a small display of tasting it and quickly approves it. Once we've all been poured a glass, Rocco holds up his.

"To you, Auntie. We're so happy with the work you've done. You hear such horror stories of builders who only do a half-assed job or never meet a project's deadline, but you finished half a day early, and definitely didn't do a half-assed job. Thank you for being so reliable." He turns to Katherine and offers her the widest smile. "You're in business with a very reliable breed," he says.

"Thank you both." Katherine winks at Rocco then holds her glass out to me. Her red fingernails stand out to me again. What is it about her nails and makeup that gets under my skin so much? "For everything."

"With all this praise, you'd start thinking I did this job for free. You are paying me, aren't you?" I joke while quickly lifting my glass a fraction. I don't hold it out any farther to clink rims with them for fear my hand may be trembling too much.

"Of course, the usual family rate," Rocco says.

"What's your next job?" Katherine asks.

If she's going to ask me direct questions, it'll be hard to stick to silence.

"I'm not sure yet. When you've been out of commission for a while people forget about you." I shrug. "It's normal when you've had to say no a couple of times. But word will spread soon enough. Builders are always needed and there are never enough of us to make people's renovation dreams come true. It's how the world turns."

"Sounds like a very good profession to be in," Katherine says. "What made you become a builder? I guess it's more common now for a woman to choose that profession, but I can imagine that back in the day, it must have caused some looks."

"I still get plenty of looks." I take a sip from the wine, which is light and crisp and just the way I like it. "But I worked with my father for a long time before I took over his business when he retired. You tend to run into the same people a lot." I lean back in my chair. "Clients are something else, of course. The majority hardly bat an eyelid when a woman turns up on their doorstep, but some really can't deal with it. And then there are those who don't notice I'm a woman at all." I throw in a chuckle.

"We all have to live in this world," Katherine says. "Which is rife with prejudice." She locks her gaze on mine for an instant. Is she trying to send me a message?

"That may be so, Kat," Rocco interjects. I'm surprised he's managed to let us speak for this long without intervening. "But Auntie Hera made sure I was ready to face any prejudice when it was time to come out. Plus, she made my coming out to my parents a piece of cake."

I wave off Rocco's comment. "Your mother knew long before you did."

"And in all fairness, darling," Katherine adds, "you've worked in a gym for most of your professional life. Being gay is practically a requirement for an instructor in a Bondi gym." She gives him a smile that lights up her face.

"What is this?" Rocco says. "I was trying to have a genuine heartfelt moment and all I get is the lezzers ganging up on me." He sighs dramatically. "I've always vehemently fought what Auntie Hera has told me all my life. That of all the variations of gender and orientation, gay men and lesbian women have the least in common, except the battles we've had to fight side by side. Right now, for the first time ever, I'm starting to believe you were right." He paints on a smirk.

I can't help but laugh at his silly indignation. Rocco has always had a knack for making a point in the most dramatic fashion. He gets that from his mother, for sure. Sometimes, when he was at my house as an adolescent, it was like being around my teenage sister all over again.

"Then I guess we should toast Hera once again," Katherine says. "For encouraging you to become such a fabulous and unapologetic gay."

"What's there to apologize for anyway?" Rocco says, before taking a sip of wine.

"Absolutely nothing, when it comes to your sexual preference, at least." I glance at Katherine. It was quite fun to gang up on my nephew for a minute, to jest with another woman like that.

"What do you mean by that exactly?" Katherine asks. Her gaze is glued to mine. "By the 'at least' in what you just said?"

Chapter Eleven

KAT

"I'M NOT sure I know what you're getting at," Hera says.

"I think it's wonderful that you've been such a great role model for Rocco and I appreciate that coming out was much harder a mere decade ago, let alone thirty years ago. But how can you sit here basking in Rocco's praise about you being so supportive when, all the while, you're judging me?"

Damn. I didn't mean to have a go at Hera. She hardly deserves it. In fact, apart from the clear judgment she's been casting on me since the very first moment we met, I can so clearly tell she and Rocco are cut from the same good-natured cloth. But it's perhaps that one glaring discrepancy in her personality that gets to me. Moreover, this is supposed to be a happy occasion. Us thanking her for a job well done, and celebrating another milestone in our journey toward our coffee shop dream. Yet Hera can't help but ruin the moment with her snide little remarks. If she thinks she can just keep dropping them into conversation, and hope Rocco and I won't notice, she has another thing coming. Granted, Rocco probably doesn't notice, but I do. I'm too finely attuned to throwaway remarks like that venomous 'at least' that sprang from her lips.

I might be able to understand people's reactions to what I do—we all live in the same world, governed by the same old conservative societal rules, after all—but that doesn't mean I have to let everyone walk over me, least of all someone like Hera, who knows better than most what it feels like to have public opinion against you.

"Because one has nothing to do with the other," Hera says, casually, as if it's the most sense-making sentence ever spoken.

"Now, now, ladies," Rocco says. "Look, lunch is coming. I understand we're all a little *hangry*, what with all the hard work we've been doing. But salvation's on the way."

Our dishes are brought to the table and, as I glance at Hera, I can almost see the wave of relief that washes over her. If she thinks she's off the hook, she is, however, sorely mistaken. But I'll let her have a few bites of her lamb chops first.

"Delicious," Rocco says. "How's your salmon, Kat?"

"Good." My tone's clipped. Too clipped. I look at Hera, and how she hesitantly cuts off a chunk of lamb. I'm probably radiating combativeness. I need to defuse the situation. "I'm sorry, Hera," I say. "I was feeling a little under attack and my claws came out. It's a gut reaction."

Hera waves her fork in the air. "You and I may not agree on certain things, but we have the boy to consider." She nods at Rocco. "He's lived such a charmed life, let's not break the spell."

"Oh, great," Rocco says. "For the record, yes, I want you two to get along for my sake, but that doesn't mean you have to gang up on me and spout half-truths about me to do so."

"Make your choice already," Hera says. "I've told you many times. You can't have everything you want in life." I realize I actually haven't seen her smile yet, not the kind of genuine smile she draws her lips into right now. It lights up her face and transforms her into another person. Maybe that's who she was before Sam died. Or maybe that's the kind of person she is when she's not having lunch with former escorts.

"Tell me honestly, though, Hera." I put my cutlery down. "Would you really take on the job of remodeling my kitchen? Or were you just nodding your head to get rid of me?"

Hera inhales deeply. "Truth be told, I had no intention of actually taking on the job." That's all she says.

"*Had?*" I ask.

"I don't think I deserve the way you just spoke to me, but, then again, I don't think you deserve the way I've been speaking to you either. So let's call a truce and see where we go."

"That would be nice." I pick up my knife and fork again.

"Hallelujah. Praise the lord," Rocco says. "I've been thinking about your kitchen, Kat," he continues. "Shall I run a few ideas by you?"

"Let's see how the coffee shop looks first. Then we can talk again."

"Oh, you'll be dazzled, girl. It'll be so pretty; you'll want to spend every waking hour in the place." He quirks up his eyebrows.

"I'm very excited for you two," Hera says, "in case that wasn't clear. And very honored to have been able to help build your dream."

"Come in any time for that coffee on the house." I look Hera in the eye while I remember the only half-decent conversation we've had—those five minutes we spent chatting in the garden chairs in the corner of the Pink Bean.

"I will." This time, she aims her real smile at me, and something inside me shifts.

Chapter Twelve

HERA

"HAVE you thought more about what we discussed last time?" Jill asks, not beating about the bush.

"I always think about what we discuss. Isn't that the point?"

Jill sends me a smile followed by a gentle nod. "The job at your nephew's coffee shop is done?"

"Yep. As great as it was to work for him, I'm glad it's behind me."

Jill doesn't say anything. No surprise there.

"I'm very grateful that he asked me to do this. I missed work much more than I was willing to admit. It's great to be out there again."

Jill nods.

I wasn't going to discuss Katherine any more, yet I feel compelled to. "The three of us had lunch today and, um, some things were said." It's as though I can feel the pang of anguish that burst inside of me when Katherine spoke to me the way she did all over again. It took me by surprise so much; I didn't have the wherewithal to come up with a proper reply.

"Such as?" Jill asks.

"She basically accused me of being a bigot."

Jill draws up her eyebrows.

"I may have let a few things slip. It's hard not to…"

"When you feel such contempt for someone?" Jill leans forward and places her elbows on her knees, regarding me. I know this pose. I'd best be careful what I say next, although, judging from the pose, Jill has already figured me out. It sometimes irks me how she reads me so easily, and draws conclusions about me long before I can.

"Contempt?" I meet her gaze.

"That's how I understand it. Being accused of bigotry is usually the result of displaying contempt."

"I wouldn't go as far as calling it contempt."

"What's contempt other than lack of respect for another human being?" Jill's coming on a bit strong today. It's unlike her.

I narrow my eyes as I remember her words from the very beginning of our sessions together: we are not friends. Yet I ask, "Everything all right with you?"

"Of course." She leans back in her chair.

"If you say so."

"Don't deflect, Hera."

"I always believed it wasn't your place to judge and I just felt rather judged by you."

Jill nods and purses her lips. "That wasn't my intention. I apologize."

"Apology accepted." I've lost my train of thought and am not immediately sure how to continue.

Jill re-crosses her legs. "I've been thinking about last week's session as well."

"Have you?" In all the time I've been seeing Jill, it's the first time she's said something like that. I imagine she must think about her clients, but this is the first time she's put it like this.

"What you told me about Katherine piqued my curiosity so I did some research on lesbian escort agencies." Jill states this so matter-of-factly, as though it's something people research all the time. Maybe they do.

"Did you now." Despite my disgust for the profession, my curiosity is piqued as well.

"It's an intriguing subject," Jill says.

"Maybe. In a way."

"You're not curious at all about how it all works?"

"No." I shake my head for emphasis. "But I am curious about *your* curiosity."

"So you don't mind if I share some of my findings?"

"Of course not."

Jill clears her throat. "I came across an interview with the owner of a lesbian escort agency in England. In Manchester or somewhere like that. It was very enlightening." She pauses a moment before continuing. "I understand where the mind goes when you hear the word 'escort' and the associations it immediately conjures up. Exploitation. Illegality. Human trafficking. The unsavoriness of paying for something as intimate as sex. But that's not all it is. Especially not when it comes to escorts who only work with female clients."

"I can imagine that's the picture the madam of any brothel wants to paint," I deadpan.

"For some of the clients, it's the only intimacy they experience—the only form of intimacy they have access to."

"How can you even call it intimacy?" I ask.

"Because that's what it is, no matter the exchange of money. It's a service. Touch is so important. Imagine never being touched again."

"I can imagine it very well. In fact, it's my preference," I blurt out.

Jill nods. She probably has me exactly where she wants me again.

"You may think it's your preference, Hera, but the majority of people need this basic intimacy. Leave them unfulfilled for too long and people just wither away."

"I haven't been touched in quite some time and I'm doing just fine. No urges to call on the services of an escort agency just yet, thank you very much." I know I sound defensive, and this is the last place for me to be in defense mode, but Jill's pushing my buttons—and she knows it.

"So, you can look me in the eye and honestly tell me that you haven't imagined touching Katherine?"

My eyes go wide. "I'm really worried now, Jill. It sounds to me as though you're starting to lose your mind."

"I can assure you I'm completely sane." Her gaze on me is piercing.

"I admitted before that I think she's an attractive woman. Way too glossy for me though. Why is all that make-up required, anyway? Isn't that catering to the male gaze?"

"I vividly recall you telling me that Sam liked her lipstick and mascara."

"She did, but… that's different." My voice breaks a little. "That was Sam." Just like that, the void her death left me in envelops me again.

Jill doesn't say anything for a few minutes and nor do I for fear my voice will break even more.

"Could it be,"—Jill's voice is so soft, I can barely make it out over the hum of traffic outside—"that Katherine somehow reminds you of Sam?"

I shake my head with vigor. "God, no. Sam was an entirely different person than Katherine. For starters, she wasn't a prostitute!" My voice shoots up.

"I mean physically. The way she dressed and how she

liked to put on make-up, pretty herself up before you took her out on a date?" Jill insists.

"No," I repeat.

"Okay," Jill says. "But will you think about it? We can come back to this next week."

"I can usually guess where you're trying to go with something," I say, "but the direction of this conversation is leaving me completely stumped." I shake my head again. "Katherine has nothing to do with Sam. And Sam's dead."

"Will you see her again?" Jill asks. For a split second, I think she's referring to Sam and I'm ready to declare her mental—again. Then I realize she's talking about Katherine.

"At the opening of the Pink Bean. I thought about making an excuse not to go, but Rocco will never stand for that, so I guess I'll be going."

"I think it's good that you'll see her again," Jill says. "But let's move on, for now."

Chapter Thirteen

KAT

"THIS IS IT, K.Jo," Rocco says. He stands in between Chris and me and squeezes both our hands. I'm happy for him that he gets to share this with his partner. Not for the first time since I quit the agency, I feel a twinge of something, a sadness, at not having a significant other to share such a momentous occasion with. "We're about to open for business."

I glance around our coffee shop. One wall is made up out of a huge vintage shelf unit. Books fill the open spaces, easily accessible for our customers to peruse while they have their coffee. Plant baskets hang from the ceiling, adding a green touch.

I've been to Rocco and Chris's home often enough to know that Rocco has great interior design taste, but I'm blown away by the intimate atmosphere he's been able to create. I'm proud that he's my partner in this venture—and he'll have a way with the customers, for sure.

"Let's do it. Let's open that door, darling." He gives my hand another squeeze and kisses me on the cheek.

I head to the door and unlock it, then open it wide.

We've invited our friends and families for a first-day opening party. We've had a sign outside for the past week announcing it so we're hoping some people from the neighborhood will drop in as well.

Kristin has graciously lent us some of her staff from the Pink Bean in Darlinghurst, so Rocco and I can mingle instead of making coffee. Our real test will be tomorrow. Today, we celebrate.

I glance out the window and spot a familiar red truck parked in front of the shop. Hera's. Has she been waiting for the door to open? How eager. She looks to the side, out of the open car window and our eyes meet. I give her a smile. She's not dressed in her usual worse-for-wear T-shirt, but has donned a bright white shirt with a very stiff collar. From where I'm standing, it looks brand new, as though she bought it for the occasion.

She sends me a small smile back, then gets out of the car, a bunch of flowers in her hand.

"Hi." I'm not sure how I feel at seeing her again; all I know is that I feel something. Probably just nerves because she's the first person to arrive. "You're very punctual."

"Yeah." She shoves the flowers into my chest. "I figured it'd be best to get here before the crowd does."

"Thanks, Hera. These are lovely." I hold the flowers away from me to admire them.

"Congratulations," she says. Her mouth closes, then opens again, but no more words come out. She gives me a quick, rather cold pat on the shoulder, and heads inside to greet Rocco, who's squealing and jumping up and down in delight.

I walk to the back room where I put the flowers in some water. This is just the storage room, but even here Rocco has worked his magic and made the shelves look pretty by applying some funky wallpaper to them.

"It's all in the details, Kat," he said. "And if you can choose between having a smile on your face when you get something from the shelf or not, wouldn't you always opt for the smile?" He'd beamed a wide smile at me then.

When I come out of the storage room into the coffee shop, Hera's still the only one there. It's not even two o'clock yet—the official time we put on the invitation. I join Rocco, Chris and Hera.

"It's really gorgeous, Rocco," Hera says, and I can hear the pride in her voice.

"Can I get you a coffee?" I ask. "Or something stronger, to mark the occasion?" I smile at Hera. She looks different after she's gone all soft as a result of her nephew's accomplishments.

"A glass of champers for Auntie Hera, of course!" Rocco shouts. "I'll get it." He heads behind the counter, to the large fridge which, for the occasion, is stocked with bottles of bubbly. Chris follows him, leaving me alone with Hera.

"Are you on your next job?" I ask, to fill the silence.

She nods. "A remodel just a few blocks away from here, actually."

"Ah, will we be seeing you around for a few cups of black coffee then?"

"Maybe. If I forget my flask," she says matter-of-factly.

I can't help but chuckle. This is one of the happiest days of my life and just a minute ago, Hera herself was radiating happiness for Rocco, but a few moments alone with me seems to have returned her to her usual self—at least the self she has chosen to be when she is around me.

"What's so funny?" she asks.

"You really don't like me, do you?"

"It's nothing personal. Really," Hera says.

"That's a good one. Of course it's personal. It usually is when you don't like someone."

"Maybe you're used to everyone liking you all the time, but I'm not. It's not a big deal." Hera turns away from me a little.

"Maybe you can recommend someone else to renovate my kitchen then," I say, my tone a little menacing. I'm fine with not being liked by everyone—which only puts me at an even keel with the rest of the human population—but I'm not fine with Hera raining on my parade, today of all days.

"Sure."

Rocco and Chris return, each with two glasses of sparkling wine in their hands. They hand one to both me and Hera.

"To the Pink Bean," Rocco says.

"To the Pink Bean," I repeat, pride swelling inside me.

Hera and Chris join us in a toast. I decide to forget about Hera's negative vibes. This is my and Rocco's day. This is our dream, one that has come true well ahead of the vague planning we always entertained between us, sometimes more as a way to fill conversation than anything else. Then Jessica introduced me to Kristin and now here we are.

I check my watch. It's a few minutes past two and there's movement outside. A few people walk past the window. They're all women.

"The guys had better arrive soon before I wither away from too much estrogen around me," Rocco says.

Chris bursts out into a chuckle. Hera's face remains expressionless.

Kristin's the first to walk in. She has seen the place already, of course, but she still takes a moment to admire it—for the sake of her company.

Sheryl heads straight toward us and throws her arms wide. "Congratulations, Kat, it's so gorgeous."

While she hugs me, I take in the women who have walked in with her. "Caitlin and Jo are here."

"Yes, and be warned, Caitlin's on a mission," Sheryl says, as she lets go of me.

"What kind of mission?" I ask.

"You'll see." Sheryl winks at me and greets Rocco.

We are all introduced and I try to remember all the names—Micky, Robin, Amber, Martha—but more people walk in and soon all the names I've heard are a blur and our party's on.

———

"I know your gut reaction will probably be to give me an immediate no," Caitlin says. "But try to respond, not react." She beams a sly smile at me.

"She's been spending too much time with Amber," Josephine says. "Too much meditation isn't always a good thing." She kisses Caitlin on the cheek.

"What is it you're trying to lure me into?" I ask.

"I would be extremely honored if you'd be a guest on my show," Caitlin says. "I'm so sick and tired of interviewing 'famous' Australians. You, on the other hand, would make the most fascinating guest."

"Me?" I hold a hand to my chest.

"Don't be coy now, Kat. Of course you would be. You're so open and completely unapologetic about being an escort. The things you have to say would blow people's minds."

Caitlin was right. My first instinct is to give her a resounding no. "I'm flattered you would think so, but I'm also a very private person."

"I understand that." Caitlin's eyes sparkle. She has come here with her pitch prepared—and what better time to ask me than on such a merry occasion? "But the time is so right for this, Kat. I've been pushing and pushing for more radical feminist guests, and the shows have proven successful enough for me to keep on pushing. To me, you represent the epitome of feminism. I would love to get the chance to put that on display in front of a national television audience."

Jo jabs Caitlin in the arm. "I told her not to do this today," she says to me. "This is so not the time or the place."

"I'm not asking you to reply straight away. In fact, I don't want you to. I just wanted to broach the subject," Caitlin says. "So you could think about it."

"Darling." I see my friend Richard approach from the side.

"I'll leave you to the socializing now," Caitlin says. "I'll be in touch." She lightly pats my arm before turning away from me.

Richard draws me into a hug, then kisses me on the cheeks. In the far corner, I spot Liz. I wonder what she would say if Caitlin asked her for an interview. I make a mental note to speak to her in private as soon as I can.

Chapter Fourteen

HERA

"I THINK I'm going to leave," I say to Hilda.

"No, no, no," Hilda says. "I don't get to see enough of you. Besides, you've had too much bubbly. You need some more coffee before you can drive."

"I wasn't going to drive." I fish my phone out of my jeans pocket. "I was going to be very modern and get an Uber."

"I'll be damned. My sister in an Uber." She narrows her eyes. "I thought you'd feel right at home here, though, what with all the lesbians." She casts her gaze about the place. "Some of them are really hot." She bumps a shoulder into mine. "And earlier, in the restroom, I was queuing to wash my hands alongside Caitlin James." She gives a little shriek. "I just love her."

It figures that someone like Katherine would be friends with an ultra-feminist like Caitlin James, with all her talk about open relationships and sexuality. I hardly think she's a friend of Rocco's—he would have mentioned it if he was friends with the likes of Caitlin James.

"She's all right," I mumble.

"What's with the sourpuss attitude?" Hilda asks. "Ever

since I got here, you've been in a foul mood. Aren't you happy for Rocco?"

"Of course I am, Hilda. I know he's wanted this for such a long time. I even considered investing in his dream, but then, well, you know."

"You wish Sam were here to see this." Her voice is solemn.

I nod.

"I wish she were here too. She'd fit right in. She would have absolutely loved this."

I catch a glimpse of Katherine and think about what Jill asked me to consider. In our last session, I managed to avoid the subject of Katherine altogether, because I suffered one of those all too familiar falling-apart days—even though it had been months since the last one.

I picture Samantha next to me. Sometimes, when I'm alone in the house, it's as though I can still smell her. Out of nowhere, I catch a whiff of her favorite perfume, and it always knocks me for six.

"If you're taking an Uber anyway," Hilda says, "how about another glass of that champers. Not too bad for a coffee shop, I would say." She shoots me a big grin and goes in search of more. I don't even have the chance to decline. That's my sister's way with me. I've had more than fifty years to get used to it. It would feel off if she were to ask me gently if I wanted another glass of sparkling wine. Like just after Sam died, and she suddenly started speaking to me in a soft, deferential voice I didn't recognize. For a moment, I thought I had lost my sister as well as my partner.

I glance around the place. Rocco has done a great job with the interior. I get a feeling this place will be successful and I guess, for that, he also has Katherine to thank. There go my thoughts again, drifting to Katherine. Where is she now?

She seems to be fond of the color red—today she's wearing a bright red blouse. It makes her stand out. I don't even need to search for her in the crowd. She's talking to the woman who was here on the first day of my job. What was her name? Liz, I think. They're deep in conversation so I take the opportunity to watch them discreetly. Katherine shakes her head, then she tilts it and brings her fingers to her cheek, tapping just below her cheekbone in exactly the same way Sam used to do. Damn it. Maybe Jill was right.

I look away from Katherine and her friend and try to find Hilda. She has two glasses in her hands, but she has also managed to engage Caitlin James in conversation. I guess I'll have to be patient. This is one of the highlights of her day—maybe her life—so I won't interrupt her just because I'm thirsty. Besides, I'm old enough to procure my own drink.

I head to the counter and, without asking, a young woman offers me a glass. I eagerly accept it.

Before I have the chance to turn around, someone bumps rather clumsily against my hip.

"Alyssa, can I have another bottle please, darling?" I recognize Katherine's voice.

Alyssa nods and goes to fetch the bottle.

I glance to my side and it seems that Katherine only now notices how rudely she has bumped into me.

"Don't mind me." I turn the snark all the way up in my voice.

"Oh, sorry, Hera. I didn't hurt you, did I?" She looks me straight in the eye. There's not a hint of apology in her glance nor in her voice. In fact, her eyes are a little glazed over.

"Of course not," I reply.

"I can tell you're rather tough." She glances at my hips, as though that's where the evidence of my toughness can be found. She looks back up and locks her gaze on my drink.

"I'm glad you're letting your hair down a bit, Hera. We all need to have some fun." She smiles now—a smile I don't know what to do with.

Luckily, Alyssa returns and hands an open bottle of sparkling wine to Katherine. "You don't need a top-up?" she asks.

"No, thanks."

"Talk to you later," Katherine says and *sashays away*—an expression I've learned from Rocco.

I stand by the counter a while longer, waiting for Hilda to return and tell me all about her conversation with Caitlin James. I regret that I was so cold with Katherine when I first arrived. Tonight, on this happy occasion, for the first time, I can see her for who she really is—just a woman living her life. And experiencing great pleasure from doing so. Even though she has disappeared into the crowd in front of me, I swear I can hear her laugh bubbling up over the noise.

I could do with some of that pleasure, I conclude. It's been too long.

Chapter Fifteen

KAT

IT's the first operating weekday of our Pink Bean and Kristin has just left. Rocco's wiping the spout of the milk frother for the umpteenth time today. It seems to be his nervous tic. According to Kristin, we've sold a decent number of coffees for a first morning. Now that she's left, and it's just me and Rocco in the shop, it feels like our very first minutes of complete independence.

"It's strange," I say to Rocco. "All this time we've dreamed of this, and now here we are, and I don't really know what to do with myself."

"Why do you think I've been keeping that machine squeaky clean?" he says.

"It's just nerves, isn't it?"

"How about a nice cappuccino to help you with those?" Rocco grins at me.

"I wish we were still serving bubbly," I joke.

"That was quite a party."

Someone walks by the window and we both stiffen. We're not used to this yet. I consider both Rocco and myself very good with people, but it doesn't feel natural yet to have people walk into our coffee shop. We're still adjusting to the new reality of our lives. This morning, apart from being exhilarated, I was so nervous, I thought I might say yes if Alana called me again. But she has stopped calling now.

A man walks in and Rocco and I paint on big smiles.

"Hi there," Rocco says. Somehow, even on this very first morning, it has become the natural order of things for him to greet the male customers.

I try to make myself look useful by grabbing a cloth and wiping the tables I've already wiped a dozen times. Everything's in order. Everything's set up so that we can serve customers easily and swiftly. Now all we need are the customers.

Rocco and the man continue their chat. I sit at a table in the corner and, out of habit, pull my phone out of my pocket. I notice I've received a message. It's from Caitlin asking me not to forget about her proposal.

I haven't forgotten. In fact, I've had quite some time to think about it, but no matter how I twist and turn her offer of being a guest on *The Caitlin James Show*, I can't conclude that it's my task to convince the nation that sex work has its virtues.

Another person walks by the window, drawing my attention. A familiar figure. Tall and broad-shouldered. Short hair. Faded black T-shirt. Hera. I can hardly believe it. Maybe she has forgotten her flask again.

She walks in and Rocco's face lights up. I'd best go say hi. I never thought she'd actually show up.

It takes me back to the very first time she came here, when all the work still had to be done—and I was oblivious to the fact she had already made up her mind about me being a lesser person than her.

"Hi." I send Hera a smile nonetheless. "Long black?"

"Katherine," Hera says, as though stating a fact instead

of my name. A fact she has no choice but to accept. Then, out of nowhere, she returns my smile. "I would love a cup of coffee."

"You're in luck," Rocco says. "We happen to be in the coffee business."

"I'll get it," I say.

"No, no, no," Rocco tuts. "Auntie Hera's first official coffee in the Bondi Pink Bean will be prepared by her favorite person in Sydney, perhaps even on this planet." He flashes a smile and turns around to make it, leaving me to chit-chat with Hera. At least she has given me a smile to work with.

"How's the—" I start, at the same time as she starts to say something.

"You first," Hera says, accompanying her words by opening her palm.

"Just wondering how the new job's going."

"Fine. It'll take a few weeks, so you might see more of me."

Is that another smile? Has Rocco's aunt had a personality transplant? She has been friendlier to me in the last few minutes than all the times I ran into her while she was working here.

"Here you go." Rocco plants a big mug on the counter. "That should keep you going for a while."

The guy who came in earlier heads back to the counter.

"That one's mine as well," Rocco whispers, then paints on his widest grin.

"He's having the time of his life." Hera's gaze softens.

"It's all still so new and exciting." I glance over at Rocco as he chats with the customer.

"How are you adjusting?" Hera asks, surprising me again.

I gaze at her from under my lashes. She did apologize

after that little spat we had at the restaurant, but this is something else altogether. Instead of judging me, she's treating me like an acquaintance she's actually fond of.

"Very well, although I'm still not used to getting up so early."

"Nothing as gorgeous as the crack of dawn." Hera looks at me over the rim of her mug, making eye-contact.

Her eyes are light brown and her glasses have slipped off the bridge of her nose again. It can't be comfortable to wear them while tearing down walls.

"I still need to be convinced of that." I return her gaze. "Once we're truly up and running, I may let Rocco do the morning shift."

Hera looks behind her for an instant. Rocco's still chattering away.

"I wanted to say sorry again for, well, you know." She puts her mug down and looks me straight in the eye again. "For being such a bigot. You were absolutely right. I have no business judging you." Her voice is crisp, her words crystal clear.

I tilt my head. "Why the sudden change of heart?"

A blush blooms on Hera's cheeks. She shuffles a bit and reaches for her coffee mug again. Her mouth briefly opens but she doesn't say anything.

"Apology accepted," I say. As much as I'd love to make her squirm some more, it's important for me to acknowledge her message. Without thinking, I place my hand on her arm. It's what I do. I trade in touch—a habit that's hard to break. Her biceps are hard against my palm.

Hera drains her cup. "I have to get back to the job." She seems to suddenly have lost the ability to meet my gaze. "Tell Rocco I'm expecting him for dinner tonight no later than seven."

"Sure." I watch Hera swagger off. There's nothing feminine about her gait. Her long-legged strides are all about function, about getting from one place to the next without fancy.

I'm happy she apologized, but I can't shake the impression there are other things left unsaid between us. I hope she stops by again soon.

Chapter Sixteen

HERA

"CAITLIN JAMES ASKED Kat to be on her show," Rocco says. "In fact, she's as good as stalking her."

"She'd make a good guest," Hilda says, "with the life she's lived."

They both look at me as though it's vital I contribute to this conversation.

"Are you sure you want your business partner to go on national TV and announce that she was an escort for a decade? It can't possibly be good for business," I say.

Rocco leans back as though he hadn't yet considered this. He glares at me.

Maybe I've read him wrong.

"Why did you even apologize to Kat if this is still how you feel about her?" Rocco asks, waving his fork around.

"Apologized for what?" Hilda asks.

"Auntie Hera could not deal. She could not deal *at all*." Rocco says it with all the theatrics of an opera singer.

"It is a little unusual that she was a sex worker," Hilda says. She winks at Rocco. "And not everyone's as open-minded as your mother."

"Which is exactly why Kat should do the interview," Rocco says. "How will public opinion ever change if no one ever talks about it?" He shrugs. "Anyway, she doesn't want to do it… yet."

"Why not?" I inquire.

Rocco scrunches up his lips. "She doesn't feel it's her job to be the spokesperson for a profession she's left." He taps a finger against the stubble on his chin. "And, actually, she may also be protecting the Pink Bean. Although, as far as I know, Kristin didn't seem to have a problem with it at all."

"If she doesn't want to do it, she doesn't want to do it." I put down my fork. "Not everyone's after their fifteen minutes of fame." I quite admire Katherine for wanting to keep a low profile—or is that my bigotry speaking again? It's hard to tell the difference, even for me.

"You tell Caitlin James," Hilda says, "that if she's after an interview with the average woman in the street, she can call me."

"Mother, how dare you," Rocco exclaims. "You are by no means average with me as your son."

We all burst out laughing and the topic of Katherine being a guest on Caitlin James' show is forgotten, although, throughout the rest of the evening my mind keeps drifting to Katherine. To how she looked at me so quizzically this morning after I apologized. As though she was onto something I have no clue of yet myself.

———

The next day I find myself at the Pink Bean again, even though I've not forgotten my flask. When I walk in, there are two people ahead of me and I have time to study Katherine as she interacts with the customers. Her long chestnut hair is tied up in a ponytail and my gaze is drawn to her fingers.

Her customary nail polish is a different shade of red than at the opening party, but red nonetheless. I guess I already know what her favorite color is.

Rocco comes bounding through the back door. He waves at me as soon as he sees me and motions for me to bypass the queue. I shake my head.

"Hello." Katherine flashes me a big smile when it's my turn. "Always lovely to see returning customers. Same as usual?"

I nod. My conviction, that it's ridiculous to pay twice as much for a cup of coffee as what it would cost me to brew an entire flask at home, has been dwarfed by my desire to help my nephew. Or so I like to tell myself.

"Coming right up." As Katherine turns around to prepare my coffee, Rocco hands me a mug already.

"I know how she likes it. Why else would Auntie Hera be back already?" He sends me a big fat wink.

I put the mug down—the coffee is, indeed, delicious—and deposit five dollars on the counter. None of that payWave contactless credit card use for me.

"A promise is a promise," Katherine says, and slides the coins back in my direction.

"I know you're good on your promise, but it makes me feel uncomfortable not to pay." I pick up the coins and hand them back to her.

"You built this place, Hera." Katherine doesn't take the money.

"And you paid me for my efforts. That's how the world works." I look her in the eye. There's a sparkle in her gaze that makes me think she's enjoying this tiny standoff between us.

"Take the money already, Kat," Rocco whispers. "It's not as if Auntie Hera spends her fortune on clothes or anything fancy like that."

I chuckle and refocus my gaze on Katherine. "He's absolutely right."

"Fine." Katherine sighs. "But you get a free refill." She grins at me. Although I'm relieved she's giving in, I'd like to stand face-to-face with her and haggle over something insignificant a little longer.

"If you insist," I say.

"I do." Her red-painted lips widen into a warm smile.

"Thanks." I deposit the money in her palm, take my coffee, and find a spot to sit in the corner.

While I enjoy my beverage, my glance is pulled back to the counter again and again, and I ask myself when I started being unable to keep my eyes off Katherine.

A few minutes later, she stops by my table. "Ready for that refill?" She has her hands on her hips.

"I really ought to get back to work."

She plants her hand on the back of the chair opposite me. "Do you mind if I sit for a moment?"

"Of course not."

She glances directly at me and, before saying anything, sucks her bottom lip between her teeth. The sight of it moves something inside me, in a spot where nothing much has moved in years.

"Would you consider it terribly untoward if I asked you to dinner? At my place." She cocks her head. "You know, so you can have a look at my kitchen. Tell me what you think."

I burst into a chuckle while a sensation I can't identify courses through me. "I don't think it would be untoward at all. It would be work."

"Are you free this weekend? Say, Sunday?"

I nod. I'm usually free.

"Any food allergies I should take into consideration?"

"Nope. I'm old school like that."

This elicits another smile from Katherine. "I figured you

would be." She rises. "It's a date then. I'll text you the time and address."

I watch her walk off, all sass and delicious curves. Only then does it hit me what she just said. It's a *date*.

For me, it will just be work.

Chapter Seventeen

KAT

"*You* could do it," I say to Liz. "If you think it's so important. You look like a model and a movie star rolled into one."

"I wasn't asked," Liz says matter-of-factly.

"I wonder why that is." I scan Liz's face. "Jessica's no longer Caitlin's boss, so it can't be that."

"Jess's father still is, though, so let's not pretend it doesn't have anything to do with that." Liz draws up her eyebrows.

"So I'm the next best thing."

Liz shakes her head. "I think Caitlin has a bit of a soft spot for you."

An involuntary smile quirks up my lips. "I bet she does." I remember that night we shared fondly. "So tell me this. Will Caitlin James allow me to divulge the details of her own escapades with a call girl on her show?"

"Good point." Liz pulls up her shoulders. "I have no idea."

"You're just the messenger." I plant my elbows on the table.

Liz shakes her head. "No, I just stopped by for a coffee with my friend, really." She flashes me one of her winning smiles. "I honestly don't think Caitlin would have a problem talking about her own experiences. She does that all the time these days. And wouldn't you agree that hers is a voice that needs to be heard?"

"I do agree with that, but we should all be careful not to throw oil on the flame of the far-right, ultra-conservative populist discourse."

Liz makes a throw-away gesture with her hand. "Oh, please. Those people have long ago made up their minds about us." She leans over the table. "Look, I get it, Kat. It's a matter of privacy."

"Not just for me. I went on very public dates with women. What if their friends, or worse, their enemies, see me talking about being an escort on TV and put two and two together?"

"Fair point."

"Surely Caitlin must have thought about all these things. She's as sharp as they come."

"She's getting more and more radical, I guess."

"Just tell her no again from me when you see her." I shuffle in my seat. "Can we talk about something else now?"

"Sure." Liz eyes me quizzically. "Not tired of the coffee business already, are you? You can say what you want about being a high-end call girl, but the hours are pretty good." She waggles her eyebrows.

I pause. I'm not even sure I want to bring this up. But I can't really talk about it with Rocco. "What are your thoughts on Hera?"

"The bigoted builder?" Liz asks.

I chuckle and nod.

"Why do you ask?"

"I'd like her to remodel my kitchen."

"And?" Liz inclines her head.

"So I asked her to dinner at mine. Tomorrow."

"Because you want her to remodel your kitchen?"

"Is that so strange?"

"Nope." Liz shakes her head. "It's crystal clear to me. You have the hots for the bigoted builder."

I snort out a nervous laugh. Do I? I guess I can kid myself all I want, but I wouldn't have asked Hera to dinner if I wasn't at least a tiny bit attracted to her.

"She did apologize. Twice."

"We should do a double date. Jess can tell her all the ins and outs of dating a call girl."

"Let's not get ahead of ourselves. So far, she's been quite reluctant to even refit my kitchen."

"But she has agreed to come to dinner?"

"She has." I straighten my back. "And I have the tiniest of hunches that she kind of likes me back." An involuntary smile spreads over my lips.

"There's no underestimating a hooker's instinct. Speaking of. Is Alana still on your case?"

I shake my head. "She has given up all hope."

Liz glances around the coffee shop. "You have this now."

"I know. You know what's weird though? Free time in the evenings. Half the time, I have no clue what to do with myself."

"I know something you can do next Thursday." She reaches into her bag and hands me an invitation to an opening night at the Griffith-Porter gallery. "Bring the bigoted builder, if you like."

"Can we stop referring to Hera like that as of now, please?" I study the invitation. "Alyssa Myles. Is that the Pink Bean's Alyssa?"

"The one and only." Liz taps a fingertip on the table. "She's very talented. You should see her stuff. It's going to blow your mind."

"Really?" I study the invitation in more detail.

"It just goes to show, Kat. Most of us have hidden talents." She sends me a wink. "I mean, who knew you could make your own coffee?"

"I'd be delighted to attend." I ignore Liz's remark.

"Caitlin will be there, though, so beware."

"It'll give me a chance to tell her no once and for all." I put the invitation down. "Tell me, Lizzie…" I don't really know how to ask this, but Liz is the only one I can ask. "What's it like being in a long-term relationship after retiring from the job?"

"It has its challenges," Liz says in a serious tone before breaking out into a huge smile. "But more than that, it's simply wonderful."

"Jess is a wonderful woman."

"She sure is. Now *you* tell me something, Katherine Jones… Might you be on the prowl?"

"I might very well be." I smile at Liz. I want what she has with Jess. It seemed so unlikely when they first met, yet look at them now.

Chapter Eighteen

HERA

I GLANCE at myself in the mirror and run my hand over my hair. I trimmed the edges and I find myself worrying over something I usually never worry about—my hair looks a little uneven on the sides. Sam used to do this for me. She'd take the clippers in her steady hand and make me look as good as new again.

There's a picture of us on the mantle next to the bedroom mirror. It shows us in our thirties, brimming with health and as careless as we could be. Sam wasn't supposed to die four days after her fiftieth birthday. She sure as hell wasn't supposed to die without giving me the chance to say goodbye.

"What do you think, babe?" I ask her picture. "Can I go out with hair like this?"

I try to imagine what she would say but the situation makes it hard. In my gut, I know this isn't just me having a look at someone's kitchen for a possible remodel job. If that were the case, I wouldn't even have combed my hair. I wouldn't be standing in front of the mirror stressing out about something that can only be noticed if examined closely.

"It's just a job," Sam might say. And if she were still alive, then it would just be that. But now that she's been dead for more than a year, it's something else.

I turn around, facing away from the mirror and the picture of Sam and me. Jill's going to have a field day when I tell her about this next Wednesday. I can already predict her questions. I push those thoughts from my mind as well and walk to the closet. I guess a T-shirt is out of the question. Or is it? I'm not one for great sartorial debates but I realize that what I wear will send a message. If I turn up at Katherine's in one of my work T-shirts—freshly washed because it's a Sunday after all—it will tell her that this is nothing more than a work appointment. But most potential clients don't cook me dinner so I should at least make some effort to reciprocate the gesture. And then there's the small matter of what I want to project.

I've warmed to her since we first met and I can almost be myself around her without constant images of her... of her what? How does it even work when you're an escort? Maybe I should ask her tonight. But no, best steer clear of that inflammatory topic. She's Rocco's friend and business partner and she and I might become friends, but never anything more than that. That's probably the most important message to send. I accept who she is, but we can never have anything between us. Not only because she used to be a call girl, but because Sam's sudden death plunged me into such a pit of despair. I'd rather be alone for the rest of my life than experience the loss of a partner again.

That's decided then. I reach for a navy-blue V-neck T-shirt and pull it over my head. That should convey the message.

———

When I ring the doorbell at Katherine's, I wish I'd worn a shirt. But at least I've brought a bottle of good wine. While I wait, I run my finger over the nick in my hair. I hear the lock being turned and hope she won't be all dolled up—although all dolled up seems to be Katherine's default mode.

As soon as the door opens, she sends me a wide smile.

"Hi," she says, and ushers me inside. She briefly puts a hand on my shoulder and I'm happy she doesn't kiss me hello. That would be very un-work-like. Maybe we have the exact same idea about tonight. I hand her the wine while I force myself to relax a little. Then I glance around.

Katherine's apartment is gigantic even though it's just on the outskirts of Bondi on the right side to get to the city center. It must be worth a small fortune.

"Crikey." I stifle a remark about how the escort business must be very profitable. I don't want to start off the night that way. And of course it's profitable. Why else would a woman like Katherine bother? "Nice place."

"Thanks." Katherine briefly glances at the label on the wine bottle, then puts it on the table. "Do make yourself comfortable." She points at the largest sectional sofa I've ever seen and a thought pops into my head. Did she use to 'entertain' here? Did unspeakable acts happen on the very sofa she's pointing at? Surely there must be some sort of protocol—and a smart woman like Katherine wouldn't jeopardize her privacy like that.

"Shall I have a look at the kitchen first?" I ask.

Katherine cocks her head. "It's a bit of a mess at the moment. I promise you that I can actually cook, but I tend to make a right mess when doing so. I'm a bit like Nigella that way, except that I have to clean it up myself." Her eyes light up as she smiles.

"Is it going to be less of a mess at any point during the evening?" I ask.

She quirks up one corner of her mouth. "I'm afraid it will only get worse."

"Then I'd best have a look now, don't you think?"

She nods and I follow her to the kitchen. I take the opportunity to eye her from behind. She's dressed in some sort of red jumpsuit that flows around her body as she walks.

"It does look like a bomb went off in here," I say when I enter the kitchen.

"What can I say?" Katherine puts her hands on her hips the way I've seen her do a few times. "I'm a messy cook. It's my style."

I glance around the kitchen, trying to ignore the chaos of dirty pots and pans. The cabinets and work surfaces look almost new, no scuffs or scratches visible anywhere. And the appliances are all top-of-the-range as far as I can see.

"I'm not really sure why you asked me here. This kitchen doesn't need to be refitted."

"Maybe it doesn't need to be, but I *want* it done. Would that be okay with you, Hera?" She narrows her eyes.

"How old are your appliances?"

"We can keep the appliances; I just want a different feel. All this marble is so cold. I want it to be warmer, more inviting, I guess."

"You should have asked Rocco to re-design it for you then."

"I will. After all, he's made the Pink Bean look very special. But first I wanted to ask you whether what I have in mind is possible."

She proceeds to explain that she wants the cooker on the other side, by the window, and the breakfast bar removed altogether.

I've been in this business long enough to know that it's

people like Katherine, with their surplus funds and permanent need to change their interiors, who bring in the most money. During my career, I've torn down houses that were in ship-shape condition just because the owner had a recurring dream about it being totally different.

"Everything's possible, of course. But it's going to be a two-person job. I can't get rid of all this marble on my own. And I'm certainly not going to smash it to speed things up. It's too beautiful for that."

"You want to recycle my marble?" Katherine asks, hands on hips.

"I most certainly do." For a split second, I'm not sure it's actually the marble of her kitchen we're talking about. I feel a bit light-headed—I need some food in me.

"Fair enough." Katherine steps closer. "Does that mean you'll take the job?"

"Why don't you send me some pictures tomorrow, when all this mess has been cleared, and I'll have another think about it?" I lock my gaze on hers.

"You're a hard woman to get a straight yes out of, do you know that?"

"I simply don't want to make any promises I can't keep."

Katherine nods. Did she just give me a once-over? I wonder what she makes of my T-shirt. If she thinks anything of it at all, even after raking her gaze from the crown of my head to the tips of my toes, she doesn't let on. She does the mysterious sphinx smile well.

"Can I pour you some wine now?"

"Please do," I say and follow her back into the living room.

Chapter Nineteen

KAT

I WANTED this to be a date and so it feels like a date, although Hera certainly didn't dress the part. She looks every inch the builder I met at the Pink Bean a few weeks ago. A woman who is here to assess my kitchen first, and eat my food second. Most likely a woman for whom getting to know me better is the least of her priorities. It looks like I will have to deploy all the tricks in my charm toolbox tonight.

As I pour us each a glass of wine, I remind myself that this is not a paid-for appointment. This is my home and I've invited Hera for a meal because I'm so intrigued by her—although that may just be code for finding her butch and rather blunt ways a challenge as well as quite a turn-on.

"I'm glad you came," I say after I've sat down next to her, angling my body toward her. I send her a wide smile that, again, makes me feel self-conscious. I haven't been on a proper date for far too long—if tonight is even that.

"Just a heads-up," Hera says. "I have an early start tomorrow."

I can't help but burst into a chuckle. "No problem.

Dinner will be served pronto." I take a drink from the wine she brought. It's a good choice.

Hera looks into her glass, then up at me for a fraction of a second, before her glance skitters away again. "I'm… quite direct in my ways and I wouldn't want you to get the wrong idea about me."

"What idea would that be?"

"I don't know what Rocco has told you about me, but I'm not… looking for anything just because I'm single."

"Wow. You really are quite direct." I hear Hera's words but I have trouble believing them fully. Next to me sits a woman with her guard fully up, no doubt about that, but there's something else going on. Something even someone as direct as Hera can't put into words.

"I wouldn't want there to be any misunderstandings between us." Hera drinks again.

"Great way to kill the flirty vibe I was trying to nurture here." I tilt my head. "And I haven't even served you my wooing dish yet."

Hera chuckles. "You have certainly succeeded in making me very curious about it now." She holds out her glass of wine. "Friends?" she asks.

I bring my glass to hers. "A small miracle in its own right," I joke.

Hera doesn't say anything, so I decide I can play it naughty for a little longer.

"Is that why you're here then?" I ask. "To atone for your initial bigotry?"

Hera swallows hard. "And I thought *I* was direct."

"Two can play that game." I draw up my knee and it almost touches her hip.

"I've apologized for that so I thought that was behind us."

"Is it really, though?" I ask even though it's a futile question. It's a question Hera doesn't even need to answer because I can read her reply in her body.

"If it's not, then I would certainly like to put it behind us once and for all," she says.

"Does that mean you don't want to talk about it anymore or that you've fully accepted my past as a call girl?" I wouldn't have needled her so much if she hadn't tried to thwart my intentions from the get-go. What else am I going to do throughout this evening?

"It's not something for me to fully accept. In fact, it's not really any of my business."

"Would it help you if we did talk about it? If you knew more about it instead of getting hung up on all the images in your head? Most of which are, I dare suspect, based on false beliefs."

"Oh, so you can read my mind now? Very impressive." Hera shuffles in her seat and when she sits still again her hip is a few inches farther removed from my pulled-up knee.

"You're the one who toasted to us being friends earlier. I'd say, so far, the beginning of our friendship is rather shaky. I also have no intention of befriending someone who's always judging me."

Hera shakes her head. "I'm not judging you, Katherine. I'm here, aren't I? All the things you're saying to me, that you're projecting onto me, they're all in your head." She pauses but doesn't give me a chance to reply. "Yes, I was a bigot and judged you on what you used to do instead of how you were with me, which was always very pleasant. As I said before, and *meant*, I apologize for that. So why the need to drag it up again? Seems to me that you're the one who has a problem with it. Not me."

I have to put my glass down because my hand has started shaking too much. I can't remember when I last got a dressing-down like this. The hardest fact for me to grasp is that

Hera is probably right. I'm the one with the chip on my shoulder tonight.

"Okay." I rise from the sofa. "Do you mind if I take a minute before I reply? Meanwhile, I'll get dinner ready."

Hera looks up at me, her gaze not flinching this time. "Take all the time you need. I'm not going anywhere."

———

"It has been harder than I thought," I say, after we've sat down for our meal. "I've always been so headstrong about my profession and I've always been able to defend my choice but, now that I've quit, there seems to be this… I'm not sure how to articulate it. A vacuum of sorts. Like I'm no longer the person I used to be. And I still get very defensive when anyone tries to slag me off, or even hints at it."

"I, um, talked about you with my therapist," Hera says.

I nearly drop my fork. Not only at Hera's candid admission that she has discussed me with another person, but that she's in therapy. "Really?" I quickly compose myself.

"Sam and I were going through a bit of a rough spot when I started therapy. Anyway, that has nothing to do with what I'm trying to say." She waves her fork about. "Jill, my therapist, said some things about your profession that made me think. Obviously, it's very hard for me to imagine how you must feel, but I can definitely empathize with you feeling like you've lost the identity you've been clinging to for a big part of your life."

Warmth blooms in my chest. "She must be really good. Your therapist."

Hera nods almost reverently. "She's helped me a lot. Especially after Sam passed away so suddenly. But also before, when she made me realize that every single one of us is always busy reinventing ourselves and that going through a rough patch comes with the territory of change."

"You're a very wise builder, Hera." I grin at her. "You should put some of your words of wisdom on tiles like they used to do, and put them up in people's houses."

"I can do one for your kitchen, if you like." She grins at me.

"I think I'd like that very much." Hera can say what she wants about not being interested in anything romantic. Or maybe she's the kind who doesn't realize she's flirting.

"I'll have to consult Jill and see what I can come up with. No extra charge." She gazes into my eyes ever so briefly then redirects her attention to her plate. "This lamb is delicious, by the way."

"I'm glad you like it." I decide to seize the moment. "Are you interested in art at all?" I ask.

"Not hugely," Hera says matter-of-factly.

"Alyssa, the woman who was working at the Pink Bean opening, has a show in Liz and Jess's gallery. It opens on Thursday night and I've been invited. I was wondering if you'd like to, perhaps, join me?" My insides coil into a tight ball. I feel like I may have overplayed my hand—if I had a hand at all.

"Is Rocco going?" Hera asks.

I purse my lips. "I'm not sure. Liz invited me."

"Why don't you take him instead of me? I think he would appreciate it more. Art openings are really not my scene."

"What is your scene, if I may ask?"

"I don't have much of one, I guess. I prefer a simple, quiet life."

"Liz told me Alyssa is 'mind-blowingly' talented. Are you sure you want to miss that?" I quirk up an eyebrow in anticipation of her response.

"Please don't see this as a rejection, but when I come home from work, I'm usually knackered. I love what I do, but I haven't done heavy labor in quite some time and I turned fifty last year. What time does it even start?"

"Seven-ish, I guess." She's giving me an opening. "I can check right now. The invite's in the kitchen."

"If you can guarantee I'll be in bed by ten, I might be swayed."

"I hereby solemnly swear you'll be tucked in at nine fifty-nine. I'll drive you home myself."

"You're going to drive me?" Hera's voice drips with disbelief. "Do you mean you won't drink anything at all?"

"If I'm driving you, then that will be the case."

"How about I drive *you*?" She tilts her head. "That suits me more."

"Are you doubting my driving skills?"

"I doubt everyone's driving skills."

"Except your own?"

"I have nothing to doubt about my own." Hera's lips curve into a smile. If this isn't flirting, I surely must have lost the hang of it years ago.

"Come on, Hera. I'll pick you up and drive you home. Give me a chance to at least prove that I can negotiate a car through Sydney traffic."

"All of that so I will redo your kitchen?"

"And perhaps give me the number of your therapist." I reflect Hera's smile right back at her.

"I'll never give it to you. It would be a conflict of interest."

"Why?" I put my cutlery down because I'm done with my lamb—the evening has taken that kind of turn.

"Because I'm already seeing her."

"And that means none of your friends are allowed to see her?" I straighten my back.

"I think so. There must be some sort of code."

I shake my head. "I'm sure there's a code of ethics, but I'm also pretty sure there would be no mention of friends seeing the same therapist. How could there ever be enough of them if not?"

Hera leans back. "It would make me feel uncomfortable, I guess."

I pause. Hera has polished off most of her dish. "I have to respect that, then."

"I can ask Jill for a recommendation."

I nod while I sink my teeth into my bottom lip. "So, can I pick you up on Thursday then?"

Hera doesn't say anything, just nods her confirmation.

I refill our wine glasses—she hasn't said anything about driving herself home tonight so she must trust certain taxi drivers' abilities—and hold mine up to her the way she did at the beginning of the evening. "Friends," I repeat her words, although, to me, at this stage of the night, they have a very different meaning.

"Friends," Hera says, and clinks the rim of her glass against mine. "The kind you see on those silly TV shows, you know, who go to art galleries together." Out of nowhere, she sends me a wink that, if I hadn't been seated, would knock me to my knees.

Chapter Twenty

HERA

JILL SITS there with a slight smile. I haven't even said anything apart from hello. I'm still not sure why I mentioned her to Katherine, why I divulged that particular piece of very private information about myself. I know very well that these days it's almost trendy to discuss one's mental health issues—like a badge of honor—but I'm not in the habit of discussing this part of my life.

"I'm waiting for you to start," Jill says. "I sense you may have a thing or two to talk about. Something exciting."

I shake my head. When I saw my sister yesterday, a woman I've known my entire life, she didn't bat an eyelid. She just chattered away like always, not noticing anything different about my demeanor. Or maybe I've gotten too used to hiding my inner life from her.

Jill picks up on the slightest change in me instantly, though, and it's a comforting as well as disturbing thought.

I'm not one to launch straight into a conversation about my feelings, however. I need my engine to rev up, my lips to form a few unrevealing words first. "It's been an interesting week."

Jill nods and gives me time to continue. Her office is not a place for verbal fireworks—which is probably one of the reasons I've kept on coming here for so long.

"I've, um, agreed to work on Katherine's kitchen."

"That does sound interesting." Jill narrows her eyes.

"I still have a while to go on my current job, though, but…" My engine seems all revved up already. I haven't been to the Pink Bean all week, even though I really wanted to go. But Katherine must have told Rocco about asking me to the art gallery tomorrow and I know what Rocco's like. I couldn't face his inquisitive looks, not quite yet. "I went to her home. She invited me to dinner and then…" I pause to collect myself, as though I still have trouble believing any of this myself. "She asked me to this art thing tomorrow night, even though I made it very clear I'm not looking for, well, you know, anything like that. Anything she might be offering." I'm slightly out of breath after pushing all these words from my mouth too quickly.

"And what do you think she might be offering?" Jill asks.

"For some reason I fail to understand, I think she might be… interested in me."

"And you're not interested in her?" There's that smile again, more defiant this time. As though she already knows the very thing about me that I'm not willing to acknowledge myself.

"I like her and I think I made it clear we can be friends, but no, I'm not really interested in anyone. I can't be."

"Even though you clearly *are* very interested in her." Jill draws up her eyebrows.

"As a friend. Yes. I mean it was nice to be in her company. She's very easy to talk to." And easy to look at, I add in my head.

"As a friend," Jill repeats my words.

"I know what you're thinking." I may as well call her

bluff. "Just like you always assume you know what I'm thinking." The smile I send her isn't half as assured as the one she
keeps shooting in my direction. "Yes, I like her. I admit it, but
I certainly did my best to not give her the wrong idea about
me. You know that I'm not up to a relationship, and that's
regardless of the fact that Katherine used to be a call girl."

"Let me ask you this then." Jill rests her elbows on her
knees. "Do you think you deserve credit for wanting to be
friends with her?"

I chuckle and shake my head. "Of course not."

"Since you just very boldly claimed to know what I'm
thinking, do you mind if I tell you what I am actually thinking? Or would you like to tell me first?" Her smile has
softened.

"Go ahead."

"You're different today from any time I've ever seen you
in all the years you've been coming here. There's a lightness
to you that you just can't hide, no matter how much you'd
like to."

"I haven't made a new friend in a while," I say matter-of-
factly but, as I say it, it's as though I can feel the lightness Jill
just talked about glowing inside me.

Jill nods. "Tell me about the art gallery thing then." Jill
points at the abstract painting—that comforting blob of
color—on the wall behind her. "I'm quite interested in all
things art."

"Katherine's friend Liz and her partner Jessica own an
art gallery somewhere in Potts Point. They're showing art by
one of the baristas who works in the Pink Bean coffee shop
in Darlinghurst."

"Would this be the Griffith-Porter gallery?" Jill sits up a
little straighter.

"I think so, yes."

"I go to all their openings. I love the work they exhibit.

It's always right up my alley and surprisingly affordable, considering Jessica's pedigree."

Jill has lost me and… did she just infer that she might be going to the same event? "Do you mean you'll be there tomorrow?"

"I had planned to go, barring any emergencies. I usually don't work on Thursday evenings."

I shuffle nervously in my seat.

"Does that make you uncomfortable?" Jill asks.

I purse my lips. "I think it's logical that it would. I'll be there with Katherine and I'd feel… watched."

"Sydney is a big city, but that doesn't mean I don't sometimes run into clients in social situations. Don't worry about it. I'm very discreet."

"I actually told Katherine about you."

Jill draws her eyebrows all the way up. "You did?"

"It came up in conversation."

"You must really like her then."

"Actually… I was meant to ask you for a recommendation. I think Katherine might be looking for a therapist."

"And you didn't feel comfortable referring her to me?" She nods. "I get that." She pauses. "I'll email you some names."

"Thanks." Now that I know Jill will be there tomorrow, my gut instinct is to cancel the whole ordeal. I have no interest in over-priced paintings and ninety-nine percent of the art I've ever seen has confounded me more than garnered any of my genuine attention.

"Please don't cancel your date with Katherine because I'll be there," Jill says quite sternly. "You now know beforehand so it won't come as a surprise."

"How does it work when you run into clients?"

"It depends. Some people don't acknowledge me at all, with some I just exchange a knowing glance. Others may even introduce me as their therapist, while most seem comfortable referring to me as an old friend. It's never really a big deal."

I sigh. "Maybe not to you."

"I can't make you promise me anything, Hera, but I urge you to not make a problem out of this." She locks her gaze on mine. "Cultivate your friendship with Katherine. It'll be so good for you."

I find it impossible to hold her gaze for very long because, even though my brain is telling me I should absolutely not go, my heart knows that Jill is right. Getting to know Katherine has already been better for me than I could ever have imagined.

Chapter Twenty-One

KAT

WHEN I RING Hera's bell, I can't help but wonder what she'll be wearing. She did put on a shirt for the Pink Bean opening, but maybe her professional pride played a part in that.

Her house is in Bronte and looks immaculate from the outside, with flower pots gracing the window sills.

When the front door swings open I say, "Your carriage has arrived, my lady."

Hera grins at me, then looks over my shoulder. "Don't tell me you're taking me somewhere in that white thing over there." She shakes her head.

Before I reply I take in her attire. Not only has she donned the same kind of pristine white shirt that she wore at the Pink Bean opening, but she's wearing a light gray blazer over it.

"I thought red was more your color," Hera says. "But here you are, with a white car and a blue, what do you call it..." She points at my jumpsuit.

"I like all the colors of the rainbow."

Hera nods. "Have you eaten?" she asks.

"Do I look like a woman who forgets to eat?" I bring my hands to my hips.

Her cheeks turn pink. "I—I meant, do you want to come in or head off straight away?"

"I'd love to come in." I pause for a moment. "How did you know the white car was mine?"

"I know the cars in my street. None of them are white." She steps back to let me into a narrow hallway.

Hera opens the first door on the right and ushers me into the living room. I take in the wooden cabinets along the wall, the worn leather sofa and matching armchairs that stand upon a thick patchwork carpet. The room is decidedly small —especially compared to my open plan home—but it somehow feels cozy, rather than cramped. Like you'd want to curl up in the sofa with a mug of cocoa and a book, and forget about the outside world. I imagine it served as a safe haven for Hera after her partner died.

"You have a lovely home," I say as my gaze settles on her.

"Do you want to see my kitchen for inspiration?" She grins at me.

I want to see everything, I want to say, but don't.

"Would you like some water?" she asks and gestures at the sofa. "Sit for a second. I'd like to, uh, discuss something with you before we leave."

I settle in one of the armchairs and wait for Hera to return with a glass of water for the designated driver.

"Don't freak out," she says, after she has sat down in the chair opposite mine. "But Jill, my therapist, is going to be there tonight."

"Really?" I tilt my head and, just in time, refrain from making a joke that might not be received very well.

"It's a coincidence. I didn't ask her to come or anything." Hera gives a nervous chuckle that is very unlike her.

"Why would you?"

"I'm just a little bit annoyed by it."

I can't help a smile from spreading to my lips. "Because you talked about me with her? And now there's a good chance she'll meet me?"

Hera nods.

For a woman who has been on her guard since we met, she can be surprisingly open about things. I doubt she realizes what kind of signals she's been sending me. Whether she's aware or not, I'm receiving them loud and clear.

"Would this evening be more comfortable for you if I let you drive?" I give her my warmest smile.

She smiles back. Her eyes sparkle at me. "No way, I want to see you in action. If I don't like it, I'll just take a taxi back."

"I promised you'd be home before ten and I'm a girl who keeps her promises." I narrow my eyes. "Always."

"Let's be on our way then." Hera rises. "If you can talk and drive at the same time, maybe you can tell me some things I really need to know about art on the way."

———

"It's not really about the art," I whisper in Hera's ear. "It's more like a social gathering, but don't tell Liz I said that."

"I actually really like this." We're standing in front of a dreamlike depiction of the Sydney Opera House. "Don't ask me to explain why, but it speaks to me."

"You don't need to explain. And I agree, these are really good."

"Hello stranger." I feel an arm on my shoulder.

"Caitlin." I turn to her. "You remember Hera? Rocco's aunt?"

"Yes, of course. Lovely to see you again." Hera flinches a little as Caitlin kisses her on the cheek. "I have a bone to pick with you, Kat. I get the feeling you've been dodging my calls."

"I asked Liz to give you my message. Clearly you haven't received it."

"I have, but I've thought of a different angle." She looks over at Hera. "I don't want to monopolize you tonight, but if I come over to the Pink Bean next week, do you think we can talk?"

"A different angle?"

Caitlin gives a slight nod. "I'll tell you all about it over one of your delicious coffees. Let's say Monday?"

A waiter comes by with a tray of champagne flutes. Caitlin and Hera both grab one while I ask for a glass of water.

"Sure. Monday it is."

"I've bought two already." Caitlin nods at the paintings. "They're stunning." She cocks up her eyebrows. "Obviously I've known for a while that many a barista has a hidden talent."

"Speaking of," I ask. "Where's Jo?"

"At a gig." Someone comes along who taps Caitlin on the shoulder and she excuses herself.

"My sister said to refer Caitlin to her if she's so desperate for an interviewee," Hera says with a smirk on her face.

"Hilda?" I laugh. "She'd be an excellent guest, as would her son, by the way."

As if he has heard our conversation, a dramatic voice booms from behind us. "KJo!"

"Brace yourself." I find myself whispering in Hera's ear again, breathing in her scent as I do. "The gays have arrived."

Richard squints at Hera and me. "Wait," he says. "Is there something I should know?" He looks at his partner

Alan. "Has Rocco been keeping crucial lesbian intel from us?"

I try to wave off his comments as discreetly as possible—I'd like Hera to stay for a while.

"Lovely to see you, Hera." Richard winks at her.

"Don't mind him," I say. "You know over-excited is his default mode."

"Evening," a voice I don't recognize comes from the side.

"Jill." Hera snaps to attention—as though the head-master has just arrived to break up a raucous assembly.

"We're going to circulate," Richard says. "Catch you later."

"Bye, darling," I say absent-mindedly, as I focus my attention on Jill.

"This is Katherine," Hera says, her voice stiff.

"Lovely to meet you." Jill extends her hand and smiles warmly at me as she looks straight into my eyes—maybe she's trying to assess whether I will end up hurting her client. "I won't keep you, but I just wanted to say hello." She aims her smile at Hera now. "Have a lovely evening." With that, she saunters off and dissolves into the crowd.

I turn my body fully toward Hera. "That's done then." I glance at her empty glass of Champagne. "How about another tipple?"

"I can't believe she just came up to us. She promised me she'd be discreet."

"If first impressions are worth anything, I'd conclude she makes for an excellent therapist." I put a hand on Hera's shoulder. "I guess she doesn't let you get away with much."

"She's wonderful, actually."

Is Hera leaning into my hand?

"Ah, just what the doctor ordered." I grab a glass of Champagne off a passing tray and give it to Hera.

"What kind of doctor are you to prescribe me this?" Hera's voice has relaxed again.

"One without a degree but with a lot of wisdom from the streets." I glance at Hera as she takes a sip. I wish there wasn't a crowd of people around us—I wish we could continue this conversation somewhere a little quieter. From the corner of my eye, I see Kristin approaching. I remove my hand from Hera's shoulder again. "Here comes our silent investor. Lucky I'm not drinking. She can't help but inquire about 'some numbers' every time she sees me."

Kristin and Sheryl arrive and, as expected, Kristin immediately engages me in conversation about the Pink Bean. I try to give her most of my attention, but I can't help glancing at Hera as she chats with Sheryl. She nods thoughtfully and from this angle, with her chin turn downward like that, she looks so together, so every inch the woman I've come to know—serene though always a touch reluctant—that I feel something flutter inside my rib cage.

Chapter Twenty-Two

HERA

KATHERINE KNOWS MOST PEOPLE HERE, which is good. The way she's been busy talking to this and that person, tonight can hardly be construed as a date. I've had my fill of chit-chat for one evening and, as Katherine gets swallowed by the crowd more and more, I gravitate to the edge of it. I end up near the painting of the Opera House again and examine it in more detail.

"How about I replace the one you've been looking at above my head for years with that one." I instantly recognize Jill's voice.

"I think you might be too late." I point at the little red dot that's been stuck over the price.

"Oh well, guess you'll have to make do with the same old abstract then."

"Just as I've made do with you for so long," I blurt out. I've not gone as easy on the free champers as someone who has to wake up at six the next morning should.

"It's quite helpful for me to see you in a social situation," Jill says. "It gives me more context to work with."

I turn to face the crowd. Even though she's not wearing

red tonight, it's always easy to spot Katherine. "What do you think of that particular piece of context then?"

"We only exchanged a few brief words, but Katherine seems thoroughly lovely. Very warm and engaging."

"To be continued next Wednesday, I guess." It must be the Champagne, but I can't tear my gaze away from Katherine. There's something so magnetic about her.

"You bet," Jill says, and snaps me out of my thoughts about Katherine.

This is *not* a date—apart from Katherine driving me home later. Earlier, I was impressed with her driving skills. She's very assertive yet polite in traffic, which is a trait not given to many. Of course, she may very well curse like a sailor when she's alone in the car.

"I'm about to say my goodbyes, Hera. It was great seeing you," Jill says.

"You're leaving already?" I'm a little jealous of Jill. I wish I could slip out discreetly with her, but then I couldn't keep watching Katherine as she mingles effortlessly.

"I've seen what I've come here to see. I'm not one to linger." Jill turns to me. "Saying good night at these things is always a little awkward, isn't it?" She tilts her head. "Peck on the cheek for your shrink?"

"Go on then." I grab Jill by the shoulders and kiss her on the cheeks—a whole new way of saying goodbye to her—but I've had enough Champagne to not feel too self-conscious about crossing the invisible boundary we've always had between us.

"See you soon," Jill says. "Have a little fun tonight."

Jill leaves me standing there on my own, my gaze, once again, only drawn to one person.

———

"Where did Jill disappear to?" Katherine asks me as we walk to the car. It's only quarter past nine so she has plenty of time to get me home before my self-imposed curfew.

"She slunk off while you were being the belle of the ball. Isn't Alyssa a colleague of yours in a way?" I ask. "Did you ask her if you could steal her thunder on her big night?"

"I did no such thing." Katherine gives a loud cackle. She slides her arm into mine. Her body radiates heat onto me. "How dare you even insinuate something like that." She presses herself against me. She might not have had a drop of alcohol, but she must be one of those people who get intoxicated by the company of others, who come alive under their gaze.

"I was just giving you my objective observations of the night."

"Does that mean you were keeping an eye on me, Hera Walker?"

Jill's last words ring in my ear. *Have a little fun tonight.* "Some people have a knack for drawing the eye."

"Some people certainly do." She leans into me again, finding my ear, the way she has done several times this evening already. "Some of whom, well, one in particular I must say, looks rather stunning in a gray blazer."

Unfamiliar heat swells inside me. I wish Katherine would keep her distance but, at the same time, I wouldn't mind her lips staying close to my ear for a while longer.

"You mean Richard? That did look like a rather well-tailored blazer." We have arrived at the car but Katherine doesn't let go of my arm yet.

"Deflections, deflections," Katherine says while squeezing my biceps. "Goodness." She rubs her thumb over my upper arm. "I think I just found something else to compliment you on."

"The clock's ticking." I grin at her so broadly, she must

know how much I'm actually enjoying the way she's talking to me.

"Oh yes. The lady has a curfew." She lets go of me, unlocks the car, and holds the passenger door open—another brand-new experience for me.

Once in the car, Katherine concentrates on the road. Traffic's still pretty dense. I trust her driving more now that we're on the way back and I let my head fall back against my seat, enjoying the buzz of the alcohol and the warm, exciting glow of sitting next to Katherine.

"I'm glad I came," I say. My inhibitions have been lowered by the alcohol so I don't stop myself from saying exactly what I want to say—and doing exactly what I want to do.

I put my hand on her knee.

Katherine glimpses sideways for a second and flashes me an encouraging smile.

We drive the rest of the route to my house in silence, my hand firmly pressed to her knee.

———

When Katherine parks the car, I withdraw my hand. She's a swift, confident parker and the car is neatly in its spot in no time. My bedtime might be fast approaching but, even though I have a million reservations—and about a dozen reasons to bolt out of this car—I don't want to.

"Thanks for being my plus one." Katherine smiles again, but her smile tells a different story now. It tells me what I've known for a while. "I promised to tuck you in, so…" She unbuckles her seat belt.

I chuckle, then swallow hard. I hesitate. I'm almost over-come with the urge to lean in and kiss her, but I'm a woman in her fifties. I don't kiss girls in cars.

"All right then. Come inside," I say.

Katherine stands only an inch away from me as I unlock the front door. Once inside the house, I'm keenly aware—possibly helped by all the Champagne I knocked back—that I might never feel like this again. As though the exact circumstances that have been created—me being a little tipsy, being encouraged by Jill, and being intoxicated by just enough booze *and* Katherine's irresistible glow—might never happen again and I have to do something to mark the occasion.

I have to kiss her.

We're still in the hallway when I turn to her. I take her hands in mine and look her in the eye.

"You are such a remarkable woman."

Katherine doesn't say anything. She just stands there looking so incredibly alluring, with her hair a little wild, and her lips a glossy red. I take a step closer and bridge the distance between us. I tilt my head and inhale her scent—again. My level of intoxication grows. All throughout the night, it hasn't been the Champagne that has been clouding my judgment. It's Katherine. With her self-assured, inviting ways. The curve of her hips. The sway in her step. How she greets people with a warmness that's been lacking in my life. I'm drunk on Katherine and, despite all my reservations, I have to kiss her. There's no other way.

I press my lips to hers, only for a brief moment at first. During the split second when I pull my lips back from hers, already brimming with desire to touch them against Katherine's again, I realize there will be no way back from this. No way back from her body heat and the promise it holds. I kiss her again. I have to. My knees buckle when I first feel her tongue slip into my mouth.

Katherine frees her hands from my grasp and brings them to my chin. When we break from the kiss—still chaste, still exploring—she looks into my eyes and, ever so slowly, sucks her bottom lip into her mouth, her tongue flashing over it before it disappears. I forget everything I've made her stand for in my head. Desire explodes inside me. This will not end with a kiss. It's like a lid has been lifted and all the feelings I've denied myself for years, all the things I've tried to talk about with Jill but could never really find the words for—burst through the opening they've now found. The opening Katherine represents.

I walk us to the nearest wall and push her against it. When our lips meet again, our tongues do the same, and it's the kind of kiss that makes time stand still for its duration. I push my entire body against Katherine's, wanting to absorb her heat, her humanity, her very essence.

She wraps her arms around my neck and pulls me closer —although there's nowhere closer for me to go. Her hands are in my hair, my own hands begin to caress her neck, then drift lower.

"I want you," I whisper in her ear. In my own mind, it sounds more like *I need you*. I need Katherine. She quenches a thirst I haven't allowed myself to quench for far too long. I need to touch her. Need to feel a warm body against my skin, in my hands.

"Time for me to tuck you in?" she asks.

Chapter Twenty-Three

KAT

HERA LEADS me up the stairs. I have no eyes for the decoration of her bedroom—I only have eyes for her. I seem to want her more in this moment because of how she treated me when we first met. My desire has a certain I-knew-it quality about it.

Even more surprising than Hera kissing me—although I did feel the possibility of it in the air when she put her hand on my knee in the car—is how it makes me feel. Maybe this is what I need to shake my old self off completely. To move on from who I used to be and what I used to do. The more she kisses me, the more I shed my former skin—the barrier I had to create to draw a line between what was real and what wasn't.

I used to always be sure. I used to always calculate my next move for maximum result, but with Hera, there's none of that. Besides, I think she might be in charge. Letting me drive her was one thing—I get the feeling she won't go as far as letting me top her.

She shrugs off her blazer and throws it onto a chair. She

switches on a lamp on the bedside table and it casts her in a seductive glow. She comes closer again.

Here is the woman I need. As I think it, I can't explain why, but the knowledge burns inside me like something that's been true forever. Like it's inevitable—part of nature's laws.

Then I have no more time for any thoughts at all because when Hera comes for me again, with the same intensity as she kissed me with downstairs, there's no room for anything else.

For the longest time, I haven't allowed my body to just be flesh brimming with desire. For years, I had to keep my mind in charge of the tiniest act my body performed. My body was my instrument, my livelihood. And now Hera's here to take all that away. And she doesn't know it, she may never know it, but she does it effortlessly. And I wonder if this is what I saw in her, even all those weeks ago when she didn't like me. I wonder if I didn't see this in her the first time she stepped out of her bright red truck outside the Pink Bean. That I could meet her needs the way she could meet mine. It's been vibrating in the air between us since the beginning, even when we were too occupied with all the other nonsense to even realize.

She tugs at the zipper of my jumpsuit. It's a bit tricky to open—one of the reasons I never wore it on the job—so I turn around in her embrace to give her better access. When I have my back to her, she doesn't fumble with the zipper though. She brushes my ponytail aside and kisses the back of my neck. Even if I can't see her face, I can feel her intention. Her desire comes through the touch of her lips against my skin.

A small moan escapes me. God, I want more. I want it all. I want to unearth the depths of Hera Walker. I press my behind against her to make my own intentions known. But Hera takes her time kissing my neck, as though she wants to cover every inch of it. Her tongue skates along the nape of my neck and the hot sensation blasts through me as though she's already touching me between my legs.

I haven't been kissed like this for ages. Another need of mine reflected in Hera's. Her hands slide around my waist, press me harder against her. Then they venture up and rest underneath my breasts. Her hands inch up and I throw my head back, onto her shoulder, in a gesture of complete surrender.

I revel in the fact that she's so completely in charge; it reminds me that I have no responsibilities here. Not tonight. Not in this bedroom with the faint light of a small bedside lamp and Hera's breath catching in my ear. I'm someone else in her arms.

Her hands cup my breasts and the entire expanse of my skin breaks out in goosebumps. There might be layers of fabric between us, but her hands on my breasts like that, almost audaciously, carry me into an area of intimacy I've avoided since I started working for Alana. You can't bring sensations like this to a job. It's as if Hera reads my body, as though her hands on my breasts signify much more than an erotic gesture—much more than foreplay. She's getting to know me, without words, finding the real me. Seeing me in the semi-darkness of her room.

Her hands squeeze me intimately and my nipples push against the fabric of my bra. They burn against it, wanting to tear holes through it, wanting to be touched by her desperately. Her lips skate along my neck and her kisses are no longer measured. They're wet and her tongue is in play and I can feel Hera's desire—her need—for me in the press of her body against mine. Her hands slide from my breasts to my back and she pushes me away from her. She zips me out of my one-piece item of clothing as though she deals with extremely aroused women in jumpsuits on a daily basis.

I kick off my shoes and stand in front of her in my underwear. On display, which is nothing I'm not used to. Hera's gaze is burning, like I've seen many a client's do, but this is different. I'm not the one to pounce. I don't try to get her white shirt off her. I could try but I sense that she's the kind of woman who likes to strip off her own clothes.

I suck my bottom lip between my teeth again, the way I did earlier, downstairs, when I could so easily tell how crazy that was driving her, how it made that wall around her crumble. The wall may not come all the way down tonight, but there are huge gaps in it already. The first brick was removed long before Hera put a hand on my knee in the car.

She unbuttons her shirt but doesn't take it off. Briefly, I can make out the olive skin of her belly, as she rushes toward me again, as though our separation has already lasted long enough. Her hands are in my hair, tugging at the band that's holding up my ponytail. As my hair cascades down, she looks at me as though she's just spotted the world's most beautiful hidden waterfall. The desire in her eyes is the kind no money can ever buy.

She kisses me again and walks me toward the bed as she does. Her mouth is hungrier on mine, her tongue more insistent than before. The backs of my knees hit the bed and she pushes me down, flanking me. I sense some movement in her legs as she kicks off her shoes, then presses her warm, warm body against mine. She kisses me again, all intention and heat, then pauses and gazes at me from above. No words are needed now. I don't have any of my own and if I did, I wouldn't say them, because I wouldn't want to break the magic spell of this moment. The warmth in Hera's eyes, mixed with the desire demonstrated through her actions meeting my own, is plenty to rev up my engine some more. My clit already aches for her touch. I want her strong, sturdy builder's fingers inside me. God, I want them so much. But I need to go at her pace. I need to give her this moment. Mine will come later because, even though I'm fully in the throes of my own desire, a part of me already can't wait to see Hera yield under my own touch.

She kisses me again and it's a kiss that doesn't stop for minutes. While her lips are locked on mine, Hera draws a line with her finger from my chin, over my neck, to my breast. It dips underneath the cup of my bra, finding my nipple. I bring a hand underneath Hera's shirt, my fingertips scratching the skin of her back. As her body presses into me, so does her belt buckle, but I restrain myself and don't try to undo it and get it off her. If it leaves a mark, it's one I will look at with nothing but fond memories.

Hera pushes herself up, the side of her shirt covering my belly. Her finger withdraws from my bra as she finds her balance, then she brings both her hands behind my back to take off my bra. She doesn't say anything but I can see the wonder in her eyes when my breasts are bared to her. As though she had resigned herself to never seeing another woman's breasts in the flesh again. I could be wrong—I could be reading Hera all wrong—but that's how it feels to me in that moment. Like I'm a miracle Hera never even dreamed to hope for ever again.

I glance down as Hera comes for me, both her hands on my breasts. There's hunger in her grasp, something untamable. Her true nature coming through that carefully constructed wall, pushing through, telling her that this part of her still exists. This particular moment of wonder I've seen many times and, every single time, it fills me with hope and gratitude and I marvel at how humans can deny themselves something so essential. But, no matter how adept we become at ignoring our needs, they always find a way to shine through again. It's no different with Hera and the eagerness in her grasp is reflected in the pulsing of my clit.

And anyone who has ever tried to argue with me that what I did was just sell my body, sell the naked act of sex in exchange for money, has never witnessed a moment like this.

I need to snap myself out of this train of thought. Hera looks up at me briefly, as if she knows I'm on my own personal journey as well, and I send her a small smile of encouragement, to let her know that I'm with her here, all the way.

She leans her head down and while her hands try to contain my ample breasts, she sucks my nipple between her lips.

"Oh," I moan, and rake my fingers through her short hair. Hera licks and sucks and, then, bites down gently. My body sizzles with the heat that's being generated between us. Her lips sear against my nipple, erasing all the memories that have no relevance tonight. Because tonight, I'm here with Hera, and this is more real than anything I've ever known. It holds more promise and gives me hope that, maybe I too, can be destined for love.

Hera's wildness increases. Her lips on my other breast are less restrained. She pushes me all the way down, her hands sliding from my chest over my arms to my hands. She intertwines her fingers with mine, then kisses my breasts again. Her tongue flicks over my nipples, her teeth graze against my flesh. Then, she finally makes her way down.

I can't help but squirm against the sheets. My legs are already spread for her, but I'm still wearing my panties. Not for long though. From Hera's breathing, I can tell she's past the patient, teasing stage. I can tell she wants to lick my clit as much as I want her to lick it. She aches for me the way I ache for her. And even though, on my way over, and throughout the hours we spent at the gallery, I didn't even allow my mind to entertain the possibility of this for a fraction of a second, maybe the hope brimmed somewhere inside me nonetheless.

Hera kisses my inner thigh, inching ever closer to my panties, which have become a nuisance now. The last frontier before I give myself to her completely. And I want to give myself, I'm ready. I want to give myself in a way I haven't in a very long time. No holds barred and, also, without a whiff of transaction to it.

Hera kisses my belly, just above my panties. I push myself toward her—my way of giving permission, or, perhaps, of telling her to get those wretched panties off me already. I want to be naked for her, show myself unrestrained, meet her growing wildness, her desire to please me, with everything I have—as my truest self.

Hera's losing it as much as I am. She tugs at my panties now, showing her unbridled self to me in the process. We're matched, I think, in this moment of desire, of nothing else but our need for each other, perfectly cast in the roles we're in.

Hera sits between my legs, looking down at me. I only see the crown of her head but her gaze on me there is enough to set my skin on fire. She bows down, her body folding in on itself, and then, at last, I feel her breath on my swollen lips.

She kisses my inner thigh again but without the barrier of my underwear between us, the sensation is much more urgent, much more paralyzing. Because now I am at her mercy. I want her to do this to me.

Her lips reach my clit. She kisses it tentatively, but only for a split second. Then her tongue comes out to play and I'm lost. I disappear in the joy her touch brings me and it's no longer just her tongue on my clit that I feel, it's all her intentions, and all my own desires bursting through my flesh, straining under the surface of my skin. I'm as alive as I've ever been as I allow this very sensation, this surrender to another person completely, back into my life.

And god, I want her to fuck me, but I'm so aroused, my desire is so acute, that I'm not sure my body has the patience to hold out. And why would it wait, when it has waited all this time? Surely, this is not a one-night thing between us. It can't be. Most likely, it won't even be a one-orgasm night. What with the way my flesh is coming alive, and desire is crystallizing into pleasure on my skin. Hera licks and sucks my clit into her mouth. I rock my pelvis up to her, to her eager, able mouth; I press my hands into her hair pushing her as close to me as I can bear. And then I come because there's no sense in waiting, in denying myself this burst of pleasure, this wave of nothingness and everything that takes me, and tethers me to her in a way I someday hope to adequately convey to her. But for now, I collapse under her touch. I free myself from who I was and become someone else with her—as we are always a slightly different version of ourselves with different people.

I cave in under the pressure of her tongue, of how it feels to be naked in front of her, opened up, vulnerable but safe in the knowledge that she knows what to do with me.

"Oh Christ," I groan, and pull Hera toward me hurriedly. I look into her eyes briefly and before I pull her in for a kiss, I wonder if that was the beginning of a tear in her eye.

Chapter Twenty-Four

HERA

I WRAP MYSELF AROUND KATHERINE, feeling nothing but honored that she's allowed me to drink her in like that, to take from her so freely the thing I wanted the most. For the privilege of burying myself between her legs.

She pulls me close to her and I rest my cheek on her chest. God, those beautiful, luxurious breasts. I fear I may never get enough of them. I wouldn't mind lying like this for the rest of the night. But first, I fear, there's a conversation to be had.

"Do you feel all tucked in now?" Katherine whispers above my head.

I nod, her breasts swaying with my movement. I don't feel like lifting myself toward her, like facing her. I need this moment of quiet bliss, of her hand gently twirling through my hair, of the up-and-down of her chest beneath my cheek.

But I don't want to take too many liberties either. And what do I really know about what a woman like Katherine's thinking? All I do know is that she just came under my touch, and the power of that is unrivaled in what my life has become since Sam's death.

Katherine's hand wanders down my back, her finger tracing a line down my spine over the fabric of my shirt. She cranes herself toward me and kisses the top of my head. "I know it's way past your bedtime now," she says, "but let me give you something that will make you sleep like a baby." Her body shudders underneath me as she chuckles.

Her hand has traveled up again and her fingers dig into my shoulder.

"Hera," she whispers. "I'd very much like to kiss you again."

The prospect of Katherine kissing me is too alluring to resist. I push myself away from her chest and peer into her dark eyes. She looks like a different person lying in my bed like this. Her hair is wild, her gaze is full of something I haven't seen in it yet. And she's naked, of course. And newly recovered from a quick, inevitable orgasm.

She looks a bit like Sam.

I quickly push the thought from my mind because it feels so wrong to bring the memory of Sam into this situation.

"Come here," Katherine whispers, and pulls me close to her. I can still smell her on my lips and my mind drifts back to that glorious moment when my tongue met her clit for the very first time.

She kisses me, her lips hot and silvery against mine, and I lose myself in this kiss, the way I've been losing myself since I pushed her against the wall downstairs.

"Can I take this off you?" Katherine asks, taking the collar of my shirt between her fingers. "I feel a bit naked next to you."

"Let me." I sit up and shoulder off my shirt. "Better?"

"It's a start," she says, "but I'm still feeling a little under-dressed." She throws in a smile. "Or do you sleep in those jeans?" She quirks up an eyebrow.

I don't immediately react.

Katherine tilts her head and, in the low light of the room, finds my gaze. "Are you all right?" she asks. Her voice is gentle, not a hint of insistence in it.

"I'm perfectly fine." I try to sound light. "What just happened between us was magic as far as I'm concerned, but... erm, I'm not sure I can reciprocate in the same way."

Katherine narrows her eyes. I can see her swallow hard. "Do you mean you feel uncomfortable getting undressed in front of me or... do you mean that you prefer not to be touched?"

"Both," is the only word I can push past my throat.

"Come here." She opens her arms wide.

I scoot closer to her again, and to be held by her with so much skin on skin contact is divine in its own way, but it does nothing to change my mind about what I want.

"Here's a suggestion," she whispers. "Show me the way to the bathroom and while I'm gone, you can undress and wait for me under the covers." She kisses the edge of my ear. "If you want me to stay, of course. Do you want me to?"

"I'd like that very much," I quickly confirm.

"I'd like that too." She slides down until we are face-to-face. "I happen to quite like you."

"You're just saying that so I give you a good price for redoing your kitchen."

Her lips curl into a half-smile. "You see right through me." She plants a kiss on the tip of my nose. "Where's the bathroom?" she asks.

I show her the way and fall onto the bed after she has left the room. I ask myself if this is some sort of defining moment for the rest of my life, but I don't have time to answer that question—no matter how valid or silly it may be —while Katherine's in the bathroom. I promised I'd undress while she was out of the bedroom, so I'd best get on with it.

I step out of my jeans and dispose of my underwear,

throwing it in the laundry basket in the corner. While I'm at it, I hang my shirt on the back of a chair and find Katherine's discarded clothing. I fold it, underwear included, and put it on the same chair.

I feel no need to hastily duck underneath the covers because this is not really about being naked. I'm too old to have many qualms about my body—and your partner suddenly dying rather puts having a patch of cellulite on your thigh into perspective. It's only when the door to the bedroom opens that I throw the duvet back, inviting Katherine underneath it with me.

Her gaze flits over my body and when she meets me in bed, gluing herself to me immediately, I see desire glimmer in her eyes.

"Do you want to talk?" she asks, her face so close to mine that her breath warms my cheeks.

"Do you feel like we need to talk?" I ask.

She chuckles and I feel her breasts—nipples all perked up —shake against my skin. "I guess that means no."

"Look." I create a fraction of distance between us. "It's not that I don't know how to do all of this anymore, because I do—"

"I noticed," Katherine says with a loopy grin on her face.

"Emotionally, I mean. Well, not just emotionally, but…" I'm not sure I have the words to explain this. Not now, after a night out—after going down on Katherine. "Maybe we can talk tomorrow?"

"Can I ask you one question?" Katherine's face is more earnest now.

"Of course."

"Is it your intention to make a pillow princess out of me?"

I can't tell if she's being serious or not, until she bursts into a giggle.

"I'm not going to lie," she says. "After the life I've lived, I could probably get used to that." This makes her laugh so hard, her entire body rocks.

I can't help but laugh with her. Jill will have some work to do after so recklessly advising me to have some fun.

"For your information, my alarm clock goes off at five-thirty," I say.

"Looks like I won't be getting my eight hours of beauty sleep then." Katherine pushes herself against me. "Heads-up, my complexion might be a bit off in the morning."

"I look forward to meeting the early-morning you." I kiss her on the cheek. No matter how the evening has ended, it was still one of the most amazing nights of my life. "Do you want to be little spoon or big spoon?"

"I wouldn't for a second consider being the outer spoon, Hera," Katherine says, and turns around in my embrace, so I can pull her backside close to me.

Chapter Twenty-Five

KAT

I WAKE UP, it seems, only a few minutes after I fell asleep. Hera's clock radio crackles way too loudly in my ear. Hera. Memories of last night flood my brain and I blink open my eyes.

"Sorry about that." Hera leans over me and gives the alarm a good whack. She breaks into a smile while she squints. "Are you related to Katherine Jones?" she asks. "You kind of look like her, but also not quite like her."

"Whatever happened to good morning, my love?" I groan.

"Morning." Hera leans in and kisses me on the lips. "Did you get some sleep?"

"Not enough."

"Don't you have to open the Pink Bean?" she asks, an amused smile playing on her lips.

"Rocco's opening this morning. I told him I had a big night planned."

"What, getting his aunt into bed by ten?"

Hera looks a thousand times more relaxed than last night, when she didn't want me to touch her. It makes me wonder if I should make a move now. But it's early and I think it's a safe bet to leave the making of moves to Hera for now. "Which I did, by the way. Mission accomplished."

"Did you tell him you were taking me out?"

"No, but I'm pretty sure he knows by now. The gay gossip mill never stops turning. I'm willing to bet Richard texted him within minutes of seeing us together." I pause. "Do I need to watch what I tell him?"

"Heavens, no. He has certainly never watched what he's told me about his love life. All the things he didn't want to discuss with his mother, he has always, very graphically, discussed with me." Hera scrunches up her face.

"Are you giving me permission to tell him I spent the night with you?"

"He's your best friend, Kat." It's the first time Hera has called me Kat. "And I trust you know where to draw the line." She cranes her neck and looks at the clock. "I really need to get going. But feel free to linger."

"How about I make you some breakfast while you shower?" I bat my lashes.

"I must have died and gone to heaven." Hera pulls me in for one last hug, and I soak up all her warmth. I'm not sure when I'll get the chance to savor it again.

———

By the time I arrive at the Pink Bean, it's almost ten. I've stopped by my apartment to change my clothes and make myself presentable.

Rocco's busy and just gives me a look. I jump right in and work alongside him, only exchanging coffee-related words with him until the queue in front of the counter has dissolved.

"You sure took your sweet time this morning, K.Jo." He steps back and crosses his arms in front of his chest.

I try to disarm him with a smile. "I'm so sorry, darling. One of those mornings."

"I'm not going to be all coy with you about this. Hera is my aunt, Kat. Why didn't you tell me you were going out with her?"

"I thought you were sulking because I was late."

"I can handle a crowd." He leans against the counter.

"I didn't want to make a big deal of it beforehand. To be completely honest, I sort of expected Hera to cancel on me last-minute."

He takes a step closer. "I'm just… very ambivalent about this," he whispers. "She might not look it, but Hera's fragile."

"I can handle fragile."

"Oh, I'm sure you can, but, on top of that, you're mixing business with pleasure. What if things go wrong between you? Who will be caught in the middle then?"

"I think you might be getting a little ahead of yourself." I can understand Rocco's defensive attitude up to a point, but I hadn't expected him to come down on me so ferociously—even though, most days, ferocious seems to be his default mode.

"Just…" The door swings open. He leans in and hisses, "Don't hurt her, Kat. I swear to you." Rocco greets the customer and I'm left standing there baffled. Maybe the Walkers are a much more complicated bunch than I thought they were. I've known Rocco for years and he has never spoken to me so disrespectfully.

"For your information," I say, once the customer has left, "Hera and I had a lovely time. Maybe, instead of throwing a hissy fit, you could be happy for us?"

"I'm not throwing a hissy fit. But we are here together every day and you didn't breathe a word of it."

"Because it's delicate. She *is* your aunt and I know you adore her."

"She doesn't have many people. I can't help but be protective of her. She's only just now started coming out of her shell again. You weren't there when she…" He falls silent.

"Look at it this way." I try a smile. "If your beloved aunt's going to go on a date with someone, wouldn't you prefer it to be with your best friend instead of someone you don't know the first thing about?"

Rocco just stands there, nodding slowly. "That's the thing, Kat. I'm not so sure."

"Excuse me?" I have to restrain my indignation—I sure hope Rocco didn't mean what I think he meant by that—because the door opens again. My heart skips a beat because it's Hera walking in. She has some plaster on her cheek, and her hair is all dusty, but she looks scrumptious just the same.

"Hi." She saunters up to the counter and sends me a big smile, then glances over at Rocco, who still has a pout on his face. "I'm not sure which vibe you're going for today, but I sense some tension in the air," she says matter-of-factly. "I sure hope I'm not the cause of it." She sends me a wink.

"Long black, Auntie?" Rocco asks, not acknowledging what Hera has just said.

"Yes, please."

"On it." He turns away and starts preparing the coffee.

"Some of us are not having the best morning." I lean over the counter and kiss Hera on the cheek.

"Does he have a stick up his ass over us?" Hera asks.

"I think, perhaps, he feels a bit left out," I say.

"I can hear you, you know," Rocco says.

"Good to know there's nothing wrong with your hearing then," I quip. "Only your loyalty to your best friend."

"Rocco," Hera says. "Come sit with me for a minute." She winks at me again. "I'll sort him out," she whispers.

Rocco takes her coffee to the table furthest away from the counter. I'm still shocked by what he might have implied about me but, now that Hera's here, I trust he'll see things differently soon enough.

Chapter Twenty-Six

HERA

I LOOK AT MY NEPHEW. Even though he's a grown man, I can still see the child in him.

"Great coffee." I look around the place. "Good number of people in here, as well." I take a sip. From the moment I left my house this morning, with Katherine still inside, I knew I wouldn't be able to stay away from the Pink Bean today. I knew I had to see her again as quickly as possible.

Rocco chuckles half-heartedly. "I don't need a talking-to in case that's what the two of you are thinking."

"I wouldn't dream of giving you one." I lean over the table. "Instead, let me tell you all you want to know." A warm tingle spreads through me as I remember the sequence of events. "Kat invited me to hers last Sunday to have a look at her kitchen. We had a lovely meal. Then she invited me to Alyssa's art show at the Griffith-Porter gallery, and we had a great time." I suppress a giggle. 'Great time' sounds like the understatement of the century.

"I know all about the great time you had. Richard sent me a picture of you and Kat at the gallery." He sighs. "I'm not upset because I didn't know. Although I probably should have known, what with the way I'm always up in Kat's business. Nor is it that she didn't tell me about your dinner, which I've only just found about. In fact, it's great that you get along now." He briefly purses his lips. "Let's be honest, that never really looked as if it was ever going to happen, did it?"

I shrug and take another sip from my coffee.

"It's just that… now that I'm faced with the two of you together, it's really weird for me. That's the only way I can describe it." He looks over his shoulder. "From the way you were making eyes at each other, I guess you'll be seeing each other again."

"I sure hope so." I lean back and glance over at Katherine. She looks like the other version of herself again, all made-up and ready for the daytime. Already, I like all versions of her. "I know I didn't give her a chance in the beginning. I was clearly wrong. She's… pretty amazing."

"It's really strange for me to hear you say those words?" Rocco slants over the table. "Not only because you're my aunt, and I've only ever known you to be with Sam, but also, well, because of the things you said about her when you started the renovation work here."

I nod. "I fully accept that." I'm not sure what else I can say. All throughout last night, from the moment Katherine showed up at my door, I've not given much thought to what she used to do.

"That's it?" Rocco asks.

"I guess so."

"I was a bit mean to her earlier." He sits up straight again. "No one needs to convince me that Kat's amazing. I've known that forever."

"Now I know it too." I shoot him a wide grin.

"Chris couldn't believe it either."

"How about you and Chris come over for dinner at mine soon?"

"That would be nice." He narrows his eyes. "If Chris hadn't had this work thing last night, I would most likely have been at the gallery myself, you know."

"Good thing you like a nice surprise then." I smirk at him.

He shakes his head. "It's really not as funny as you think it is." He has a grin on his lips regardless of what he just said.

"You're right." I drain the last of my coffee. After I put my cup down, I say, "I'm very serious about this." I look Rocco in the eye. I can tell from his slightly frustrated facial expression that there are things he wants to share with me, but has decided against. Some things are better left unspoken. "I need to get back to work. I'll give you a call soon." I get up and stand next to him. I put an arm on his shoulder and give it a little squeeze. "Thanks for looking out for me," I say, "but I'm plenty old enough to look out for myself."

———

"What are you doing this weekend?" I ask Kat, after we've had the same old squabble again about me paying for my coffee.

"No plans," she says coyly.

"Would you like to make some plans with me?" I ask.

"I thought you'd never ask." She bats her lashes. "Come to the back for a minute." She beckons me behind the counter.

I follow her into a small storage room, which is, completely according to my expectations, neatly organized along the principles of Rocco—he once explained them to me but being rather chaotic myself, I've long forgotten them.

She closes the door behind us and presses me against it. Her breasts push against mine and I feel the same heat as last night course through me.

"Maybe some more of this?" she whispers in my ear, before kissing my neck.

"Who can say no to that?" I push her away from me slightly. "You'll have dust all over your dress if you keep this up."

"Goodness," she coos, "imagine what Rocco will have to say about that."

"He's under the mistaken impression I can't fend for myself—or deal with a woman as wonderful as you." I gaze into Katherine's dark-brown eyes, wishing I didn't have a job to go back to.

"I'd best not give him all the details about last night then." Kat rubs herself against me again, clearly not caring which state it will leave her clothes in.

"You can tease him a little, though." I pull her in close. "He deserves it." Before I kiss her, I ask. "Tonight?"

She nods her confirmation and then our lips meet, and it's so easy to forget we're in the storage room of the Pink Bean, when Katherine is pressed against me like this, and all I want to do is tear that dress off of her. But I can wait until tonight.

Chapter Twenty-Seven

KAT

"BEFORE YOU GET any wild ideas in your head," I say to Hera after she's let me in and we're standing in the living room, a little more awkwardly than I had anticipated, "I have to open the Pink Bean tomorrow."

Hera regards me intently. "I'll make sure you get your beauty sleep."

I sigh. "I'm really feeling it." I bridge the small distance between us. "Even though my new job is not nearly as emotionally taxing, my work hours are much longer. And I don't get to have any more naps." I run a finger up her bare arm. Hera's freshly showered and is wearing a clean T-shirt. "I've always been a strong believer in the power of the nap." I grin at her.

"Would you like to take a nap while I make us some dinner?" Hera puts her hands on my hips.

"That's the problem. When I'm with you, I don't feel like napping at all."

Hera nods. "What do you feel like then?"

"I feel like doing this." I drag my fingers higher up her arm, underneath her sleeve, and witness how her skin breaks out in goosebumps. Hera might not know it yet, but I've come here to seduce her. I have full faith in my powers of seduction—after all, they were my bread and butter for years. "And this." My other hand softly brushes Hera's neck, just above the edge of her T-shirt.

I hope Hera was only joking when I asked her, in jest, if she intended to make a pillow princess out of me. I need to taste her, feel her on my fingers. Find out what she looks like after she has come.

"You're not hungry?" she asks, her breath catching in her throat.

"Only for you," I say, knowing full well how cheesy that sounds.

"I seem to have quite an appetite for you as well." Hera still has her hands on my hips and she tugs me to her. Before she kisses me, her lips curl into a small smile. She brings her hands to my back and holds me close, before going to work on my zipper. She must be really hungry then.

I let her strip me but I've come with my own agenda today. I'll let her take the reins for a while—it obviously excites her—before I make my own move.

She has my dress in a puddle on the floor in no time and has already progressed to the clasp of my bra. Before I know it, I'm standing in Hera's living room in just my underpants.

"Whatever happened to offering a girl a drink?" I ask.

"I'm not old-fashioned that way." Hera grins at me. "Also, it's a miracle I made it out of the site alive today, or without causing an accident. In fact, it should be illegal for me to go to work when under the influence of Katherine Jones."

I burst into a chuckle. Hera's desire for me is no match for my intentions. She comes alive when she has her hands on me and, in turn, it excites me beyond belief. But I will, at the very least, need her to take her T-shirt off before she goes any further. I start hoisting it over her chest, but she doesn't let me. Instead, she pulls it off herself.

She's wearing a sports bra so white, it must be brand new. It contrasts with her olive skin and I need to look away from her chest, into the bottomless pools of desire in her eyes, to stop myself from stripping her of that bra right there and then.

She presses herself against my side and launches an onslaught of kisses on my neck, while her hand already delves down. She briefly strokes my belly, her mouth meandering to my breast. As she sucks my nipple between her lips, her finger skates over my panties. I know what Hera means when she says that, all day long, she's been distracted to the point of it being dangerous. After she left the Pink Bean, I spent every free minute daydreaming about something very much like the situation I'm in—although the roles were quite reversed.

But as I stand here, it's impossible not to go with the flow Hera's creating. Her determination is sexy. The clench of her teeth on my nipples is so light in its grasp but so firm in its intention, I soon want her to rip my panties off me and slide a finger inside me. God, how I want to feel her inside me.

Her finger circles my clit, while her lips are fastened around my nipple—as though she couldn't let go of it even if she wanted to. I glance down at her strong neck, the muscles moving beneath her skin, straining to please me. Everything in her body working toward the same goal.

When she does finally let go, and she looks at me, her face is flushed, the lust in her glance multiplied.

"Come," she says under her breath, and leads me to the sofa. Before I have the chance to sit down, she tugs off my underwear and, once again, I'm naked before her while she's still half-dressed. I give her a look and she must be a fast learner. She unbuckles her belt and quickly gets rid of her jeans. Then she tilts her head as though asking, *Is this what you wanted?* A new rush of warmth spreads inside me. It's definitely a big part of what I want.

I wrap my arms around her and hold her near-naked body against mine, inhaling her scent, reveling in the touch of her hard muscles beneath her soft skin.

"Lie down for me, please," she whispers and, by now, she doesn't have to ask me twice.

I lower myself onto the sofa and Hera crouches beside me. She kisses me and I throw my arms around her neck, while she pushes my bent leg up against the backrest. I can feel the air brush my wet lips, my swollen clit.

"God, you're so beautiful," Hera says, a crack in her voice that tells me she means it with all her being. "I want you so much. It's crazy."

But then her lips find my nipple again and while one of her hands grabs hold of my breast, the fingers of the other create patterns on my inner thigh. My exposure lifts my already growing arousal to boiling point again. This is how I am with her. Easy to combust. Ready for her when she wants me. And she wants me, there's no getting away from that.

She lifts her head away from my breast and looks me in the eye while her finger zones in. She circles my clit, once, twice, ever so slowly. My breath starts to come out ragged. I want her too. Like this, in exactly the way she has maneuvered me into this position—outmaneuvered me, even. And now, my body is only desire, throbbing with impatience and anticipation, as my clit pulses under her touch.

She looks down at me, between my legs, so I only see the top of her head, and her robust shoulders. Her gaze on me there magnifies all the sensations I've been succumbing to again. Then, with that light, soft touch she has, she slowly slides the tip of her finger inside. She leaves it there, unmoving, and looks up again. It's only when her gaze is firmly locked on mine, that she pushes her finger inside of me completely.

I moan and let my head fall back a little, while still keeping my gaze on hers. My limbs stiffen with pleasure. Hera's fucking me and all the fires that I managed to dampen since she left her house this morning come roaring back to life, until, with her thumb deftly stroking my clit, they culminate into the fire to end all fires once again.

After I've come and Hera's lying on the too small sofa with me as best as our two bodies can manage, I whisper in her ear, "Hello to you too."

"Are you still hungry?" Hera asks.

"Absolutely ravenous." I'm lying on my side and pull her close to me.

"Shall I make us some dinner?" I can feel her lips move against the skin of my neck as she speaks.

"Still not hungry for food yet." I kiss her neck. "I want you." I nibble at her earlobe. "I think I've waited long enough." My hand travels down her back and halts at the clasp of her bra. This kind of model is too sturdy for me to undo with just one hand, so I try to maneuver my other hand behind her back, but we're too closely pressed together.

"Any chance we can move this upstairs?" I ask.

"How about after dinner?" she says. "I need to eat something first."

I'm not willing to let this go. Perhaps I haven't made adequately clear how much I want her—a desire she must be able to understand, what with the way she just ravaged me as soon as I walked in the door. "Then let's stay here."

"Kat," she says, and tries to push herself up. She slides half off the sofa and it seems to change the air between us, seems to transform it from electric to awkward. "Maybe later, okay?" Hera climbs to her feet and towers over me. "I really need to eat."

"Do I detect some *hanger* in the builder?" I quip, trying to lighten the quickly darkening mood.

"I've been on my feet all day, doing some pretty heavy-duty work. I need fuel to keep going." She stands there shifting from foot to foot, claiming to need food—which is a perfectly reasonable demand—but I can't seem to shake the impression that she's actually trying to say something else entirely.

"Okay." I watch her find her jeans and T-shirt and slip them on swiftly.

She crouches down and puts her hands on my thigh. "You relax for a bit. Take a shower if you like. We can talk while we eat."

I nod. She kisses me briefly on the cheek and then, barefoot and scrumptious, saunters to the kitchen.

Chapter Twenty-Eight

HERA

AFTER HER SHOWER, Katherine borrowed one of my T-shirts. It's a bit short and small for her, making her look extra desirable. Her make-up has been washed off and, all throughout dinner, I couldn't keep my eyes off her.

It's only after we've nearly polished off a bottle of wine that I find the courage to say what is almost unsayable. We've retreated to the sofa we fooled around on earlier, Katherine leans heavily into me, and I revel in the pleasure her weight against me brings. The coziness it creates. How it makes this house feel more like my home again.

"I'm, erm, not very good at being touched in an intimate way," I mumble.

Katherine does me the courtesy of staying in position—and not turning to look me in the eye.

"What do you mean by that exactly?" Her voice is only mildly inquisitive.

"It's not something that is of vital importance to me."

Katherine doesn't immediately say anything. The in and out of our breath is the only sound in the room. "May I ask why?" she says after a while.

"I'm not sure there's a why. That's just how it is." I wish I could say this with more aplomb, with more gravitas.

Katherine does turn toward me now. She pulls her knees onto the sofa and faces me. Before she speaks, she takes my hands in hers. "Has it always been like that?"

I chuckle. "You make it sound as though I have some sort of condition."

"That's not how I wanted it to sound. I'm just curious… because I like you."

It's hard to keep my hands in hers. "I understand if this is a deal breaker. That's why I'm telling you now."

It's Katherine's turn to chuckle nervously. "I don't think it's a deal breaker. I'm just trying to understand." She tilts her head. "Your partner. Sam. She never touched you?"

"She did, before…" This is an almost impossible conversation to have. I don't have the words for it. I can't even explain it to myself—despite trying many times. "It's just not a part of my life anymore."

Katherine sucks her bottom lip between her teeth the way I've seen her do many times by now. "I can't sit here and look you in the eye, and honestly tell you, that this isn't hard for me to understand." The clasp of her fingers around mine becomes firmer. "I—I want you in that way, Hera. So much. I mean, I happily gave myself to you. Very happily, but it was always under the assumption that I would reciprocate."

"Sex doesn't always have to be about reciprocation."

"I think I know that." She drops my hands and straightens her spine. "You don't have to educate me on all the things sex can be." She narrows her eyes. "It's not because I used to be an escort, is it?"

I shake my head vehemently. "No. I promise you that has nothing to do with it."

"Good." She huffs out a sigh, as though if I had even hinted at that, she'd be out of the door in no time. "Is it a matter of trust? Of going too fast? Admittedly, things have moved quickly between us once we——"

I shake my head again. "It's how I am. How I've become. Maybe how I've always been, although it's not that easy to find out."

"Do you…" She takes my hands in hers again and looks at them. "Do you masturbate?"

Even though I feel like I owe her answers to these questions, it doesn't make them easier to reply to. "No," I say.

She nods slowly. "I feel like I should be able to deal with this better, but I'm not quite sure what to say."

"It's a lot to take in, especially after I pounced on you like that… I should have had this conversation with you a lot sooner. But, um, I hadn't anticipated things progressing so quickly all of a sudden."

"That's what I have such trouble understanding," Katherine says. "You clearly feel sexual desire. You obviously want me with all that is in you. But you don't want to have an orgasm? You don't need release from all that tension?"

"I get my release when you come."

"Really?"

I nod.

"So, right now in this moment, when I'm sitting here in front of you in this T-shirt that barely covers me, what is it that you feel?"

I shoot her a grin. "I very much feel like ripping that T-shirt off you."

"And I very much feel like ripping yours off you," Katherine replies, melancholy in her glance, reminding me that, even though the conversation might have briefly taken a lighter tone, this is not the sort of thing that can be resolved just by having a quick chat.

Moreover, I have no reply to what she's just said. What could I possibly say? I surely can't take the liberty to have my way with her again—I probably should have restrained myself before.

"Do you want to watch *The Caitlin James Show* with me?" I ask. Because to me, watching TV with Katherine by my side can just as well be a pinnacle of intimacy.

"Sure." She cocks her head. "She's coming to the Pink Bean next Monday to pitch a new angle for that interview she so desperately wants to do with me." Katherine leans into me again.

"You're a very interesting woman, so you can hardly blame her."

"Don't you start as well." Kat puts her head on my shoulder and, in that gesture, I can sense her willingness to stay—to give this a shot regardless of what I've just confessed.

While I switch on the TV and find the right channel, I vow to take some time this weekend to articulate what I find so unspeakable. Katherine deserves more than what I've just given her.

Chapter Twenty-Nine

KAT

"I COULD SO EASILY FALL in love with her," I say to Liz and snap my fingers. "Just like that, actually."

"Then why don't you?" Liz grins at me.

I sigh. "It's even more complicated than I first thought."

"Isn't it always?" Liz brushes her hair out of her eyes. "Life's complicated. If anyone knows that, it's us."

"Simply knowing things are complicated doesn't really change anything about the situation."

After a long day at the Pink Bean, during which I didn't really know what to say to Rocco—except that, perhaps he was right to be worried about our working relationship if things go south between Hera and me—I remain preoccupied, unable to confide my innermost thoughts to my best friend.

This entire day my brain has been busy mulling over what Hera said last night. So much so, that I called Liz and asked her if I could stop by after work, even though what I really needed was a hot bath and a very long night's sleep.

"Do you want to tell me what makes it so complicated? Except for you being a former call girl, of course. But if that's it, let me hook her up with Jess. She can tell her all about the tricks we have up our sleeve." Liz's lips curve into a wide smile.

"That's just the thing. I'm not allowed to show Hera my tricks. Any of them."

"What do you mean?" Liz twirls her beer bottle between her fingers. "You haven't had sex yet?"

"She doesn't want me to touch her," I blurt out and, as I say it, I realize I really needed to voice that to someone else.

"I see." Liz seems stumped for words for a bit, but then says, "Like in the stone butch kind of way or because she believes you've touched too many a lady already in your life?"

I snort at the way she phrases it. I knew she was the right person to talk to about this. I couldn't possibly discuss it with any of my gay male friends—never in a million years would they understand.

"I suspect the first. Although I get a feeling it's much more than just that."

"Wow." Liz lifts the beer bottle to her mouth. "How do you feel about that?"

"I'm not really sure." I drink from the crisp white wine she has poured me. "I'm still processing."

"Perhaps it took you by surprise."

"You can say that again. The first time, I thought she was just tired, you know. Fair enough. But yesterday she told me, *after* she made love to me."

"I'm sure you've had clients like that," Liz says matter-of-factly. "I sure had my fair share of them, but I always thought it was… I don't know. Fear more than anything else stopping them from wanting to be touched."

"I don't know Hera well enough yet to work out what it is, but it is definitely a thing. And I really, really like her, and I almost feel guilty for being so dramatic about this. Like it's

untoward in some way to question someone's sexual proclivi-
ties, because maybe it is just her nature, you know. But that's
how I feel. Massively conflicted."

"You have every right to feel conflicted, Kat. You even
have the right to turn the tables on her. What if it were the
other way around? Would she continue to see you?"

"Good question." I shake my head. "I really can't
imagine it. Her appetite for me is rather… voracious." A
throbbing rises between my legs at the mere thought of it.
"Maybe it's more a question of compatibility. Like with gays.
Top or bottom."

Liz snickers. "Maybe. Compatibility is a big thing in
every relationship."

"Also… in what we used to do, seduction was one of the
main parts of what we did. To drive someone crazy like that.
I truly got off on that, otherwise I wouldn't have been able to
do it for so long, and to have to completely ignore that part
of me to be with Hera. It seems unimaginable."

Liz arches up her eyebrows. "Maybe you should seduce
her until she can't stand it anymore."

"I've considered it, but after our conversation, it would
just be disrespectful."

"Do it stealthily." A grin appears on Liz's face. "Subtly
drive her so insane she won't have another choice."

I shake my head. "That's not how I want it to be."

"I know." Liz nods. "You want to be wanted."

"It's such an essential part of who I am."

"What are you going to do?" Liz's voice has dropped into
a lower, much more serious register.

"I don't know." I shake my head. "I truly don't."

"My best advice is to talk to her again. Try to get her to
tell you what's going on in her mind. It's probably all you
can do."

"I want to keep seeing her." My tone is as insistent as the

sentiment behind my words. "It's not as if I don't have my own shit to deal with as I enter into this relationship." I find Liz's gaze. "Was it hard for you? When you started seeing Jess?"

"Not hard, but definitely strange. I wanted it. I wanted something else than what I'd grown so accustomed to. And it took some convincing because dating a hooker simply isn't for everyone. At least you need to give Hera credit for that."

"She did give me a really hard time about that."

"Try to find someone who won't." Liz snickers and holds up her hands. "I loved being an escort, but being with Jess has made me want to quit as well."

"Do you regret quitting?" I ask.

"Sometimes I do, yes. But you're probably the only one of my friends who understands that."

"My life is just so incredibly different than before. It's much busier, for starters. But it's also... is it odd to say that, at times, I miss being an escort?"

"I think it's perfectly normal," Liz says.

I huff out a sigh. "Look at us, two old hookers reminiscing about the good old days."

Liz bursts out into a belly laugh. "No one is safe from nostalgia."

"Life is strange, don't you think?"

Liz lifts her beer bottle. "And we just have to roll with the punches."

Chapter Thirty

HERA

It's Sunday and I still don't know what to do with myself. Katherine and I have only exchanged a few non-committal text messages since she got up early yesterday morning to open the Pink Bean. I can only conclude her enthusiasm for being with me has waned since we had *that* talk.

I try to go about my usual Sunday morning business of reading the newspaper extras and drinking too much coffee, but the coffee reminds me of Katherine, and I can't focus on the long reads in the weekend section.

I wonder if I should book an emergency appointment with Jill, try to move our Wednesday evening time together to tomorrow, but, as much as I appreciate her, and I believe in what we do together, I know she can't really help me.

I haven't spoken to Jill about any of my sexual issues since Sam has died—there seemed no more reason to focus on them. This is also one of the reasons why I didn't want to start another relationship. Not only because I never want to go through the excruciating, paralyzing pain of someone being taken away from me again, but also to avoid needing to have the conversation I tried to have with Katherine.

I'm happy with how I am and I don't want to be pressured into defending myself. The only conclusion I can possibly draw from this is that Katherine deserves someone who is more suited to her. I let myself go when I was with her—I practically ravaged her—and that's on me. I let myself be intoxicated by her abundance of charm, by the warmth of her flesh. And she accepted my advances under the logical assumption that all would be reciprocated.

Maybe I should try writing her a letter. Perhaps I can articulate myself better, but I honestly don't know what more information I could divulge about my inner workings. To me, this is just how it is now. I could dredge up the whole history of the intimacy between Sam and me, how it changed over the years, but, frankly, I don't want to do that. That's Sam's and my private history and it doesn't concern anyone else—not even someone I think I'm falling for.

Or maybe, I should just call Katherine. Even though the thought of speaking with her makes me nervous, I prefer it over dealing with the inadequacy of text messages. I check the clock on my phone. It's almost eleven. I know she needed a lie-in, but surely she's awake by now.

I don't give myself more time to get worked up about it and dial her number. It rings a few times, then goes to voicemail. I don't leave a message. She'll know I've tried to reach her.

After trying to call her, I definitely can't focus on the newspaper anymore. Because now I'm wondering if she heard her phone, saw who was calling, and decided not to pick up. It's a possibility.

I decide to go for a walk before I drive myself crazy at home, which is already too filled with memories of her—I can't even look at my couch without my skin breaking out into goosebumps.

After I pull a sweater over my head and glance at myself in the reflection of the window, I say, in hushed tones, "Why can't you just do it, Hera? Why can't you just give yourself to her?"

But I can't. And it may very well be the end of us.

Just as I'm about to head out the door, my phone starts ringing. My heart skips a beat.

It's her.

I pick up as quickly as I can. "Hey." I instantly go all warm inside.

"Hey, you," Katherine says. "Sorry I missed your call."

"No worries." The warmth spreading through me is quickly turning into something else. Desire.

"Was there a particular reason for your call?" Kat's tone is different. She sounds more cautious than excited to be talking to me.

"I was wondering if you wanted to get together later today?" I ask. "I understand if you don't," I add, for some reason I don't quite get. It must be the tension building in my gut, crushing that initial flash of desire.

"I do, Hera, but…" She pauses.

The tension coils into a knot.

"I need a day of doing absolutely nothing," she says.

"Okay." I should probably ask if she wants to do nothing with me, but by now, I'm afraid to.

"Maybe tonight?" she asks. "Shall I give you a call later?"

"Sure. Yes. That's fine," I stammer. As I say it, it's as though I know in my heart of hearts, that she won't call me tonight. And that, if I want to see her again, I need to force something. I need to snap out of this. "I would like to, um, talk to you. I need to say some things. Please." I'm not sure why I'm suddenly pleading because I've no idea what these things that I so desperately need to say to her might be.

"Come by tonight?" she says. There's a subtle difference in her tone—as though she wants to give me another chance. "Around six?"

"I'll be there."

"See you then."

We hang up and I realize this is not the kind of phone conversation two people who have slept together would normally have—it's the conversation of two people who have considerable doubts about whether they should be together.

———

I arrive at Kat's empty-handed. At least that's what it feels like, even though I've brought a bottle of wine. Apart from that, I only feel an inevitable emptiness inside of me. Like my brain is still hanging on to something my body already knows I've lost.

Kat hugs me after she's let me in, and it's not a quick, dismissive hug. Her arms around me feel surprisingly inviting. Maybe, with her, it's the other way around. Perhaps her body is still willing to go through the motions to counteract the thoughts swirling in her mind.

"How was your day of doing nothing?" I ask.

Kat stares at me, as though instead of making small talk, I've just asked her to resolve all the mysteries of the universe.

"It was pretty awful, to be honest." She sits and I follow her lead.

What a contrast with the last time we greeted each other, when she allowed me to be all over her only a few seconds after laying eyes on her. She's dressed down in jeans and a wide, loose-hanging blouse. I can't detect any make-up on her face.

"I guess that had something to do with me."

"Should I get us a drink?" she says, ignoring my statement. "Do you want a beer?" She gets up again and rubs her palms over her jeans.

"Kat." I reach out my hand to her. "Let's just talk."

"Okay." She sits again. "I don't really know where to start. I wouldn't exactly call myself an expert at relationships." She chuckles nervously.

"I wouldn't call myself that either," I say.

"Yet you were in one for how many years?" Kat stares straight ahead.

I angle myself toward her so I can at least see her body language. I get the impression she'd rather sit with her back to me.

"More than twenty years," I say.

"I think that makes you the expert of the two of us," Kat says.

"I met Sam when I was in my late twenties," I say. "I'm not the same person I was then. I'm no more an expert than you are."

Kat sighs. "I'm thirty-eight and I've had one relationship worthy of calling it that, even though it didn't last very long. That's it. That's all I have to show for my brief years on this planet. Maybe I'm just not cut out for relationships."

"I dare to disagree." I try to inject some lightness in my tone but it comes out all wrong—like I don't mean what I'm saying.

"The truth is," Kat says and swivels toward me a bit more, "that I have no idea what to do with this. I'm sitting here, next to you, and a big part of me just wants to break out in the silliest of smiles, just because I'm sitting next to you." She grimaces. "Honestly, Hera, if I had my way, I'd have jumped you as soon as you walked through the door. Which, even though I'm inexperienced, feels quite normal at this stage of our relationship. If we can even call it that. But I can't because you don't want me to. And I know I need to respect that, but in doing so, I have no idea where this could possibly go."

"I—", I begin, but not quickly enough, because Kat cuts me off.

"Please, I need to say one more thing." She swallows hard. "I appreciate your honesty, and I feel I need to be honest with you as well. There's no other way." She clears her throat. "When I was an escort, I met many women who were in long-term relationships in which nothing sexual ever happened. Then they ended up with me." Her voice trembles as she speaks.

I wish I had allowed her to pour us a drink now. What is she comparing us—me—to? But just as she's trying to be respectful toward me, I owe her the same courtesy. Which results in me not having anything to say at the moment. The silence quickly grows heavy between us and, tongue-tied or not, I know I need to say something.

"I didn't—" My voice breaks already. I take a deep breath. "After Sam died, I knew that was it for me. I knew I would never venture into another relationship again. For many reasons, of which you know a few. So, I guess... I think, that we both feel the same way about this. I think we both know this isn't going to work." As I speak these words that seem so final, my brain is frantically trying to come up with a solution. Some magic thought that has never previously occurred to me.

Nothing materializes. I've had all weekend to think about this. Why would I suddenly find a solution out of this impasse now?

"You have a strange way of showing people you don't want to be in a relationship with them." Kat's tone is almost venomous now. Bitter. Hurt.

"I shouldn't have let it come this far." I shuffle in my seat.

"Don't you want what we had? Even if it was ever so fleeting?"

"Part of me does," I admit. "But another part of me knows I'll never be able to give myself to you in the way you expect—the way you would always want me to. I'm sorry. I can't open myself up that way any longer."

"Why?" Her eyes are pleading and wet. "Why is it so hard?"

I can only shake my head. Because the crux of it, it seems, I'll never be able to explain to anyone else. Sam tried to understand, from the meager explanations I cobbled together—words I strung together so she'd have at least something to hold on to—but it was never a resolved issue between us.

"I'm sorry I can't give you more. I just can't." I feel as inadequate as I sound, so I get up. As far as I'm concerned, there's nothing left to say. "It's best if we don't take this any further. Best to end it now." The last few words come out poorly articulated.

"You get to decide that for us as well." Katherine stands up. "You don't even want to try to find a solution?"

What solution? I want to throw back at her. But I've said enough. I drew the only possible conclusion. It's over. I know it and I think Katherine knows it too.

"I'm sorry." I glance at her kitchen. I guess I won't be remodeling it then. "I'll stop coming to the Pink Bean. We won't have to see each other again."

"Jesus Christ, Hera." Kat's fists are balled. "You're just going to walk away? I was trying to have a conversation and you're just shutting the whole thing down?"

"It's for the best," I whisper. My heart breaks as I look into Kat's furious, sad face. How I wish I could take her in my arms—and let her do the things she wants to me.

"It's for nobody's best," Kat hisses. "But if that's how you want it." She turns away from me and walks toward the window. Her back straightens and she wraps her arms around herself.

I'd better let myself out.

Chapter Thirty-One

KAT

I HAVEN'T SAID a word to Rocco about Hera, earning me a few meaningful looks and the inevitable sexist remark, "Must be that time of the month then."

If it were anyone else, I would have opened up to him, but I can't give him a suitable answer when he asks why. Although I do know I'll have to tell him sooner rather than later.

I'll just tell him to ask his aunt why we broke up before we even got the chance to get properly started.

When Caitlin comes into the shop, I just want to disappear. I'm not interested in whatever angle she has come up with to get me on her show. I'm in the sort of mood where I want to tell her to stick her arguments where the sun doesn't shine—and to ask her to never mention her TV show to me again.

"Hello, hello." She greets Rocco and me with a wide smile. "I'll have a flat white and whatever you lovely people are having, of course."

"Caitlin, darling," Rocco says. "My mother won't shut up

about you. Will you put me out of my misery and come to dinner some time?"

"What a wonderfully passive-aggressive invitation. How could I possibly refuse?" Caitlin's beaming like she's having the best day of her life.

"Lovely," Rocco says. "Anyway, let's not pretend you've come to see me. I'll just prep your order while you have a chat with Kat."

If I had remembered Caitlin was coming over today, I would have asked Rocco to invent some sort of excuse for me. To avoid me needing to have yet another conversation I don't want to have.

"Uh-oh," Caitlin says as I sit down opposite her. "I detect a *mood*. Or is it just the Monday blues?" She cocks her head. "Things not working out as planned with Hera?"

I wave my hand. "That's over and done with already, so." I try to be stoic about it but tears sting behind my eyes nonetheless.

"Oh, shit. I'm so sorry, Katherine. That was very insensitive of me." She reaches out her hand and puts it on my wrist. "Apologies."

I inhale deeply. "It's fine. And it's for the best." I briefly look her in the eye. "Please excuse me, but I'm really not in the mood to be pitched to. And I'll never appear on your show, Caitlin. You need to let it go."

"We don't have to talk about the show." Her thumb caresses my skin.

Rocco clears his throat before putting our coffees down. I can't look at him either.

"Am I disturbing something?" he asks.

"Just give us a minute, darling," Caitlin says.

"If it's women stuff you're discussing, I don't want to know anyway," Rocco says, but from the way he says it, I can tell he knows something's up. Something else I haven't told him. He saunters off.

"You're very clearly cut up about this," Caitlin says.

A tear escapes the corner of my eye. I quickly brush it away. "Honestly, we were barely together. I'll get over it quickly." I should get over it quick enough, even though it doesn't feel like that will happen at all. But I'm just being silly.

"Do you want to talk about it?" Caitlin offers me a warm smile. "I know I'm loud and brash, but I'm a good listener. And I've seen a thing or two in my life."

I look at Caitlin and I see all she stands for, with her open relationship and her life filled with love and brimming with sexual vitality. Yet, if there's one person I know who could even begin to understand this, it might very well be her.

"Even though Hera broke up with me, I feel I gave her no choice. I feel like I made her do it so I didn't have to say the words."

Caitlin drinks her coffee but keeps her hand on my arm. She nods slowly, which encourages me to continue.

"We're both mature women who've had quite the life, you know. We were both coming at this with loads of baggage. She with losing her long-term partner and me, well, you know my story. And I thought because of that, it could somehow work, but I failed to see that Hera's reticence was much more about herself than about me. And I should have given her more time. I should have been kinder. Because now I feel like I've squandered my chances."

"Kat," Caitlin says softly. "What happened?"

"She—I—" If it's hard for me to say, I imagine how hard it must have been for Hera. "She doesn't want me. I mean, she can't bear to be touched. In a sexual way."

Caitlin nods again. "Does she identify as asexual?"

"No, I really don't think so. If she does, she hasn't said as such."

"You need to stop beating yourself up about this. It's not helping anyone," Caitlin says.

"I just let her leave. And why? Because I wasn't allowed to get her off? Maybe it's the ex-hooker in me." I nod vehemently. "It must be that. The hooker can't get her new girlfriend off."

"Here's a suggestion." Caitlin leans over the table. "How about I take you home? You're in a right state."

I sigh. "This is my business. We've only just opened. I can't just take a day off."

"Of course you can. There's two of you, remember?" She gives my wrist a squeeze. "Leave it with me." She makes to get up.

I quickly shoot out of my chair. "No," I say sternly. "I don't need anyone to do me any favors. I can take care of myself. I always have."

Caitlin holds up her hands defensively. "Fair enough. Sorry to be so 'Caitlin James' about it." She flashes me a smile. "But I mean it, Kat. You shouldn't be working. You clearly haven't told Rocco so just tell him what he wants to hear, that you're feeling unwell, and go home. I'll go with you. Let's talk about this properly." She steps from behind the table and puts a hand on my shoulder. "Let me help you." She leans in. "I believe I can."

She seems very sure of herself and I could do with some help today.

"Okay." I make my excuses to Rocco, inwardly making a promise to myself that I will call him tonight to tell him about Hera and me, once I've regrouped a little.

———

"Do you think you can accept her the way she is?" Caitlin asks. She's sitting in the same spot Hera sat in yesterday.

"No," I say honestly. "I think I'd constantly try to *fix* her."

"But that's only because you don't understand her. All compassion starts with understanding."

"Compassion? I don't want to be with someone I pity."

"Compassion is not the same as pity. Come on, Kat." Caitlin didn't come here to easily let me get away with things. "You must know there's a spectrum. All aspects of sexuality can be fluid. This includes the desire to be touched."

"It's not just that." I huff out a sigh. "It's her complete ineptitude to have a conversation about it."

"Maybe that's how you can help her." Caitlin's face softens. "I'm not saying it's an easy thing. In fact, it's hard. But worthwhile things are sometimes very hard."

"Good god, no speeches, please. Doing what I used to do, I've seen some things too, Caitlin. Yes, it's hard, and I don't want it to be. All I wanted was to fall in love."

"I'm not judging you," Caitlin says. Unlike Hera yesterday, she has accepted a drink. She circles a finger over the rim of the glass. "I'm just trying to put things in perspective."

I shake my head. "I appreciate that, but no matter what you say, Hera looked pretty determined when she ditched me, so even if I manage to look at things from a different angle, it's not going to change her mind, nor is it going to change *her*." Maybe I should look at the list of therapist names Hera gave me last weekend. I wonder what she'll be talking to her own therapist about this week. Will she be able to put it into words for Jill?

"You don't know that." Caitlin puts her glass on the coffee table and fixes me with a stare. "I don't know where you got the dream notion that the beginning of a relationship is always easy. Well, I can guess, of course. So much of our modern aspirations can be blamed on the ideals we see on television every day. But I can assure you that it's not always easy. It certainly wasn't for Jo and me."

I huff out a chuckle. "I can imagine no relationship is easy for you in the beginning. Non-monogamy can be a hard sell to someone who's falling in love with you."

Caitlin shakes her head. "It's not about that. I don't go introducing myself to potential love interests like that. What I'm trying to say is that everyone's complicated. Everyone has a story. The trick is to make your stories align enough so you can have a start together."

"I don't think that's possible for me and Hera. Would we even be having this conversation if we stood a chance? Would I need all this convincing, first to convince myself and then to convince her?"

"You don't know. You never know. There's no answer to that question. The only thing you can do is try. If you feel it here"—she puts a hand on her chest—"then you owe it to yourself to try. I can see you're hurting. I can see it means so much to you. That's why I think you should try."

"In your experience," I take a breath and lean back, "do you think there's a possibility that Hera will ever inch toward the other end of the spectrum?"

Caitlin smiles at me. "Not a day goes by that I didn't wish I had a crystal ball."

"You and me both."

"The only real question you need to ask yourself, Kat, is whether Hera is worth it. Worth the wait. Worth the possible sacrifice you'll have to make. Worth accepting how she is, now and in the future."

"Then there's the minor detail that she has made it abundantly clear she doesn't want a relationship," I say, not without sarcasm in my tone.

"Clearly, she's fooling herself. Why else was she going out with you?" She drums her fingers on the armrest of the sofa. "Chances are, Hera hasn't got things all figured out either. She's probably just as miserable as you are."

I can't help it. A small flare of hope lights up in my chest. I want to believe Caitlin, although it's mainly myself I need to believe in. In my capability to be the person Hera needs me to be. In my willingness to try.

"Should I call her?" My pulse picks up speed.

"I can't tell you what to do, Kat, but, erm…" Something glints in Caitlin's eyes.

"What?"

"If you and Hera get back together as a result of this chat, will you pay me back by coming on my show?" She laughs heartily.

"You are relentless." I squint at her. "The answer is no and will always be no."

"You can't blame a girl for trying." Caitlin winks at me.

Indeed, you can't, I think, as I start coming up with my plan to get Hera back. Or, at the very least, have one more conversation with her. I'll give her a few days. Make sure she's had her appointment with Jill, who looked sensible and kind. Maybe on Thursday, I can get Hera to talk to me again.

Chapter Thirty-Two

HERA

It's hard to walk into Jill's office, especially after she has seen Katherine and me together. It seems like a lifetime ago that we were at Alyssa's show at the gallery.

"Hera." Jill greets me with a different kind of smile. She may think she knows what I'm going to say, but then she hasn't taken a proper look at my face yet. "Sit and give me some good news," she says.

My face must be expressionless, because Jill just gives me a hopeful smile.

"There's no good news," I say. "We tried and failed."

"What does that mean?" The smile slides off Jill's lips.

"It means that Katherine and I didn't even make it through the weekend."

"What happened? You looked so full of promise last Thursday? You could hardly keep your eyes off her."

"I messed it up." That knot that coiled in my stomach on Sunday is still there, still hardening—like a harsh reminder of what I said to Katherine. "It was good for a minute or two, but then I—I just had to end it. I've said it time and time again. I don't want another relationship. Sam died. It was hard. I did the work; I grieved; built up my life again. That's enough for me. I don't need more."

"I call bullshit," Jill says. "But, please, do elaborate."

She's got my hackles up already. "Ever since Sam died, have I told you any differently?" I'm starting to get sick of everyone pretending to know me better than I know myself.

"Not in words, no, you haven't," Jill says.

"What else is there?"

"So much, Hera. So very much." She crosses one leg over the other. "I was glad I saw you with Katherine. I like to think I can read people and situations rather well and there was plenty of chemistry between the two of you. I didn't need to hear either of you speak to conclude that. I witnessed it. I felt it. So much promise. So, tell me, is it over already because you don't want to be in a relationship at all, or because you don't want to be in a relationship with her specifically?"

"Definitely not because of Katherine specifically," I blurt out. "She's amazing. She deserves much, much better than me." A lump swells in the back of my throat.

"Why? I've been sitting across from you on a weekly basis for many years now and I can tell you for a fact that you're no less than any other human I've ever met. So why, when you're so clearly infatuated with Katherine, would someone else be better for her?"

"Because…" I should have canceled the appointment if I didn't want to talk about this. "I don't necessarily think there's anything wrong with me, but ninety-nine percent of the population would disagree. Katherine included."

"Did you have a difference of opinion?" Jill genuinely doesn't seem to know what I'm getting at.

"You could call it that."

Silence from Jill now. It's up to me.

"We had… we had sex. Well, not really as far as she was concerned, I guess. I told you about this before. In the very beginning when I started coming here. I don't seem to feel any need for sexual satisfaction. It just doesn't interest me. It hasn't for a while."

Jill nods. "Of course I remember, Hera."

"Which makes me rather unsuitable for a relationship. Unless I find myself a 'pillow princess', as Katherine referred to it."

"A what?" Jill asks.

"A woman who, um, likes to receive but not give back."

"Right." Jill nods. "Well, I'm sure those women exist. There are plenty of men out there like that so why should it be any different for us?" She sends me a tight smile, making me wonder about her own personal situation for a split second.

"Maybe, but, honestly, I can't be bothered going out looking for them. How would I even find them?"

"Let's go back to Katherine for a minute," Jill says. "When you say you had sex, do you mean that some things happened between you?"

I nod and swallow. The lump in my throat makes it difficult.

"And you enjoyed being with her like that?"

"Yes."

"And, up to a point, she enjoyed being with you?"

I chuckle at Jill's coyness—I'm in desperate need of a chuckle. "She most certainly looked as though she was enjoying it." My chuckle turns into a wide smile at the memory. I take a few seconds to revel in it. In the memory of Katherine's gorgeously voluptuous body, all of it ready for me. A surge of heat shoots through me, only to die with a sad whimper because of how swiftly it all ended.

"And you didn't think you could take things from there? See where it went?" Jill asks.

"No, because that would be unfair. For starters, I'd be giving her false hope because I will never change."

"But can't you see you've changed so much already?" Jill says.

That gives me pause. I don't feel like I've changed at all. I examine Jill's face. Maybe it's sad that my therapist knows me better than my own sister. I could never talk about any of this with Hilda. It's just impossible. Just as impossible as me changing in certain ways. Or maybe I've become so entrenched in this idea I have of myself, that my mind can't even envision the possibility of change.

"You have, Hera. And I should know. I have notes to fall back on. You're nothing like the woman who first came to see me and, these days, you're also no longer the woman solely defined by the loss of her partner."

"That may very well be." I did go back to work. I did, in my own way, sleep with Katherine. "But some things will never change."

"Not necessarily, Hera."

"You've lost me." I look at her expectantly. I'm not that stubborn that I don't want to change in a way that might give me another shot with Kat—I just have no clue how to go about manifesting said change.

"Change is not a big bang. It's a slow, incremental process. It's you, showing up here every week for all these years, doing the work. It's you, taking a chance on life again by remodeling Rocco and Katherine's coffee shop. It's you saying yes to renovating Katherine's kitchen. It's you going through the process while barely noticing it. You wouldn't have gone out with Katherine six months ago. Maybe even two months ago, you wouldn't have gone to the gallery opening with her, knowing I'd be there. Ever so slowly, you're opening yourself up to more aspects of life again. You're allowing yourself to blossom again."

"Maybe," I say. "But—"

"No, Hera, no buts. Surely, you must have felt this as well."

"Of course," I admit. "Mainly because of Katherine, though. And now she's gone."

"Which brings us to the million-dollar question: do you really want her out of your life?"

"If you put it like that, then the answer is no. But, and I really do need this particular 'but'." I lock my gaze on Jill's for a second before continuing. "She said so herself. Sexuality is very important to her and I don't think she has it in her to accept me for who I am."

"How about a different kind of relationship, then? A platonic one, for instance?"

"You mean that we should just be friends?" I shake my head. "I think that ship has sailed and, well…"

"What?" Jill insists.

"I'm very attracted to her."

Jill quirks up her eyebrows. "Hera, let me tell you something, seeing as that is what you pay me to do." She throws in a smile. "Regardless of the reasons, you've been sexually dormant for a long time. Then you meet this woman who is literally sparkling with vitality and sexuality. I met her and I've seen it. It only took me a split second to come to that conclusion. Of course you're attracted to her. And, lo and behold, she's attracted to you as well. Allow yourself to enjoy that sensation. It's so much rarer than you might think."

"But that's just the thing. I can't enjoy it." The words come out almost automatically, but deep down I know they're a lie.

"I think you can."

I blow some air through my nostrils. "I thought this was meant to be a safe space. An hour per week where I can feel understood."

"It's not my job to understand you, Hera. Nor am I being paid to coddle you. My task is to make you see that you are worth exactly the same as anyone else and that, for that reason, you're entitled to happiness. For the record, I believe we've made excellent progress so far." She uncrosses her legs and leans her elbows on her knees. "Let's sum things up, shall we? You have the hots for Katherine. She has the hots for you. Tell me, what's the worst that could happen if you gave it another shot?"

"The worst has already happened." My tone isn't as insistent as before. I want to believe Jill with all my heart, but I can't see how I can do that. It's like I'm missing a step in between where my thought process is and where she wants it to go.

"But you have the power to undo it."

"I don't believe I have."

"You do if you want to." Jill grins at me. "I know you're as stubborn as they come, Hera, but you're never going to convince me otherwise. I can try to make you see these things, and ideally, I'd take more time to do so, to allow you to draw your own conclusion, but I think you might be running out of time when it comes to Katherine." Her grin softens. "If only you could sit in my seat and see what I see when I look at you. If I could have held up a mirror to you last Thursday to show you the grin on your face when you stood next to her. Don't deny yourself that any longer in your life, Hera. You've done that long enough. Don't let fear take that away from you."

"Fear?"

Jill nods. "The sneakiest, most damaging, most paralyzing emotion there is. Responsible for all missed opportunities in the universe." She narrows her eyes. "Can I challenge you?"

I shrug. "You're probably going to say that's part of your job as well."

"I want to give you a homework assignment, but I want you to start on it right here and now."

"Okay." I might as well go along with it.

"Get your phone out."

I fish my phone out of my back pocket.

"Start a new text message."

"To whom?"

"To whom do you think?"

"You want me to text Katherine?" The grip on my phone intensifies.

Jill nods. "And I'll tell you exactly what to write."

"No. You're going too far."

"I know I am. This is not professional. I'll admit that. But I also know that if I ask you to contact her after you leave here, you're going to find a dozen excuses not to."

"You can't force me."

"Of course I can't force you, but I can tell you, as someone who knows you very well, that you won't regret it. And if you text her now, she may text back before the hour is up. I can then help you with a possible reply." Jill sits there beaming a smile at me.

"But I need to think this through some more. We haven't resolved the whole—"

"This is not something you have to think through any more, Hera. This is something you need to *do*." She sends me another smile. "The best way to beat fear has always been action."

I glance at my phone. I wanted to delete Katherine's number last night, but I couldn't bring myself to do it.

Something inside me lights up at the prospect of contacting her. And having Jill guide me through the process makes it easier.

"What should I write?"

"Hi. I've been an ass. Can we talk?" Jill says. When I look at her she has a goofy smile plastered across her face. "Just kidding."

Even though this doesn't really feel like the right time for a joke, I appreciate the lightening of the mood.

"How about this," Jill says. "I miss you. Can we talk?"

My palms start sweating. "I miss you? That doesn't really sound like something I would ever text to anyone."

"You never texted Sam that you missed her?"

"She was always there. I never had a chance to miss her."

"Not even when you first got together? Before you lived together?"

"That was decades ago."

"What would you write? Put it in your own words," Jill says.

I glance at my phone. At Katherine's name in the 'to' field of the message. What would I say?

"I should probably apologize." I look at Jill.

She nods. "That would be a good icebreaker."

"Okay." My fingers tremble as I start typing.

I'm sorry for all the things I said on Sunday. Can we talk?

"Now press send," Jill says.

I do as I'm told. She was right. I wouldn't have done this on my own at home—I wouldn't have had the nerve.

Jill glances at her watch. "You can wait here until she replies, if you like. You're my last client of the night."

"*If* she replies," I say. I put my phone on the table between us. I scan Jill's face. I can't help but think she's getting something out of this as well. She has crossed the line between client and therapist, the line that she has insisted for years should always exist, twice this evening.

Maybe it was seeing each other outside of this office. Maybe she has gotten truly invested in my future with Katherine, which is either still possible or eternally doomed.

We'll soon find out.

Chapter Thirty-Three

KAT

WHEN MY PHONE lights up with a text, hope sparks in my chest. But it's Wednesday evening and this is Hera's time with Jill—which is surely a time when texting is not allowed.

I'm apprehensive when I pick up my phone. It might be Alana, giving it one last try. Or worse, Caitlin—although I think she has well and truly received the message now. It could also be Rocco, checking in on me. I know Hera hasn't been responding to his texts or calls and he's worried she'll start locking herself away in her house again.

I look at the screen. It's a message from Hera.

I read it again and again. After my conversation with Caitlin, I had planned to contact her. To ask her to meet one last time, if only to not have things end on such a sour note between us. I hadn't expected her to contact me. What should I do? Text back or just bite the bullet and call her?

I decide to call her. Perhaps I can deduce something more from the tone of her voice than from these words on my phone screen.

Who am I kidding? I just want to hear her voice. And she did say she was sorry—that's most baffling of all.

My heart beats in my throat as I call her. It rings three times before she picks up.

"Hi," she says, her voice much more assured than I had expected. "Thanks for calling." Ah, no, there's the tension.

"Thanks for texting," I say. "The answer is yes. We can talk. Whenever suits you."

"Erm." There's a pause and I hear some shuffling on the other end of the line. Or is that a muffled voice?

"Are you not alone?" I ask. I strain my ear. Is that Rocco I hear? Did he get through to her after all? Gave her a talking to? It's certainly his style with anyone else, but I can't imagine him giving his aunt a stern lecture.

"I'm with Jill," Hera says.

I only met Jill briefly, but I'd like to go over to her practice and give her a big hug.

"Is it too late to come over tonight?" Hera asks.

"No," I blurt out. I don't care that I have to get up early tomorrow. I need to see Hera. I probably wouldn't sleep a wink if we set a date for tomorrow, anyway. "Please, come over. Or I can come to yours."

"I'm still out and about. I can be there in twenty minutes," Hera says.

"Okay. I'll see you then."

"Okay," Hera says and hangs up.

———

Hera arrives seven minutes earlier than she estimated. I've been counting down. When I open the door I'm both nervous and almost beside myself with excitement.

Even though she's wearing a variation of the clothes she always wears, and they might as well be the same as the ones she wore when she was here last on Sunday, she comes across as completely different. She hasn't come to break up with me again, to double confirm her sentiments about our relationship, which makes me relax a little. But still, the things she said to me can't be un-said, and we have a lot to discuss.

She waves off my offer of a beer because she has to drive, so I present her with a glass of water instead.

I invite her to sit and force myself to sit next to her, even though my legs want to pace—at least until we've both said what we want to say.

"I was surprised you texted me during your time with Jill." I start things off.

"It was a homework assignment she didn't trust me to do at home." Hera runs a hand through her hair.

I chuckle. "Have I told you that I really like Jill?"

"Look, Kat, hm… I've had some time to think and I've had this chat with Jill and, I guess, the conclusion is that, if it were up to me, I'd like for us to try again. I mean, I don't suddenly have all the answers but I shouldn't have walked out on you like that on Sunday."

"I understand why you did. I could have been kinder and more understanding."

Hera shakes her head. "I disagree. This isn't about you being more understanding. And yes, when I came here on Sunday, a big part of me did arrive with the intention of breaking things off. But another part of me wanted to explain more about how I feel. About how I am. But I didn't do that at all. Mainly because I didn't know how, so I chose the easiest road and I just left." She looks at me with a steady gaze. "So, thank you so much for agreeing to see me. It means a lot to me."

"I've had time to think as well and it's really not all down to you."

"Well, at least we're talking." Hera's grin is almost shy.

"The past few days, I've been thinking that, increasingly,

life is all about what we are able to communicate. And I don't mean just in words." I say.

"I did a pretty bad job of communicating," Hera says.

"You have to take the circumstances into account. I probably shouldn't have said that thing about a certain type of client I had." I just want to take Hera in my arms, but I'm also reminded of what I said to Caitlin—about always wanting to fix her—which is not something I can repeat tonight.

"I'm not going to lie," Hera says. "Jill spurred me on to text you, and then you called, and now I'm here. But I don't really know what to say." There's her pleading gaze on me again. "Where do we go from here? Is only the intention of being with each other going to be enough?"

I inch a little closer to her. "Who knows what's enough? All I know is that it's a start."

Hera glances at my hands.

"I should have talked to you before we ended up in bed. It's not an excuse, but things did suddenly move very fast."

"Tell me about it. I was just driving you home and, out of nowhere, there was your hand on my knee." I try a smile.

Hera nods, as if she's guilty of something. "I just—I find you irresistible and simply feeling that way about someone has caused some serious clashes with the identity I've made up for myself."

"And what would that identity be?" I scoot a little closer still.

"I think you know." Her lips don't smile, but her eyes do. "Some kind of untouchable butch builder." She snickers. "Maybe I should start tearing down my own walls."

I burst into a chuckle because it's such an un-Hera-like thing to say. Maybe Jill put these words into her mouth. But it doesn't matter where they came from. It's the sentiment behind them that counts. Like Hera's already taking the first swing of the hammer to that very sturdy wall around her heart.

"Maybe I can help you with that," I offer.

"You might break a fingernail or two in the process." Hera's smile does curl up the corners of her mouth now.

"You can't make an omelet and all that," I say, mirroring her smile.

"I can't make you any promises, Kat. I am still who I am —who I've become. And if we do decide to see each other again, I will need you to be patient."

"I've waited for someone like you for a very long time. Patience shouldn't be that much of a problem." I reach for her hand.

"What do you need from *me*?" Hera asks.

"For starters, I'd really like you to redo my kitchen," I joke. I stroke my thumb over Hera's palm. "I need you to talk to me. That's all. And I know it's hard for you, but I need you to try."

"I will," Hera says. "Although I'm not sure I have much more talking in me tonight."

"For tonight," I say, "It's enough that you're here."

"I'd like to stay," Hera says. "I'd like to just sleep in your arms." She tilts her head and leans in. "And right now, I'd very much like to kiss you."

"Both things can be arranged." As her lips touch down on mine, I feel all the way into my bones, that Hera has taken the biggest hurdle already. She came back and showed a little bit more of herself to me. As our kiss deepens, the words I just spoke to her echo in my mind: for tonight, it's enough.

Chapter Thirty-Four

HERA

I GLANCE AT MY SISTER, my lifeline after Sam died. I don't need to tell her everything, but I most certainly want to share certain things with her.

"I've met someone." I find and hold her gaze.

"You don't say." Hilda winks at me.

"Don't tell me Rocco has beaten me to it." I expel a sigh.

"I don't need my son to tell me when my sister has got the hots for someone."

I shake my head. "I've barely spoken to you. How would you know?"

"How would I know?" Hilda feigns indignation. "I only grew up with you. I've only known you for all the fifty-one years of your life. You're still my little sister. I don't need much to put two and two together. Especially not when Rocco tells me you can't keep away from The Pink Bean." She slants a little in my direction. "Apparently he's worried about you as well."

I roll my eyes, even though Rocco's concern touches me. "I knew it."

"We're family. We have no secrets. Especially if the

woman you have the hots for is Rocco's best friend and business partner. But I'm glad you've finally found the time to tell your one and only sister." Hilda runs a hand through her long, wavy hair.

"It's still early days. There really isn't that much to tell."

"Hey." Hilda's gaze softens. "I'm glad you've met someone. You've come a long way since…"

"Since Sam died." I might as well complete her sentence. I might as well say the words that have been so hard to say for all those long, dark months.

Hilda nods. "I like Katherine," she says. "She's a good person, I know that much."

"You have no objections to your sister dating someone who used to, well"—I clear my throat—"you know." It still seems hard to say out loud, especially to my sister.

"I've known Katherine much longer than you have and I've no problem with her. She's Rocco's best friend and I trust my son's judgment."

"I should probably have done the same instead of making up my mind about her before I had a chance to get to know her."

"You shouldn't blame yourself for having a very human reaction," Hera says.

"Still. It was a crappy way to behave."

Hilda shrugs. "We all have our faults and we all make mistakes. The sooner we accept that, the happier we'll all be."

"That's very philosophical of you." I drink the wine she has poured me.

She shrugs. "When enough people die on you, you're forced to look at life differently." Her gaze skitters away. "Sam's death was a blow to me as well."

I nod. "I know."

"She confided in me, you know. She... told me things. Things that, perhaps, weren't always so easy to tell you."

"About how I wasn't always the easiest person to be around?" I can say it with a hint of a smile on my lips now.

"She certainly didn't have to tell me that." Hilda chuckles.

"Neither one of us were saints."

"She loved you regardless. She accepted you, Hera. With all your idiosyncrasies and all your ambivalence about, well, certain things."

I shake my head. Hilda may think she knew what was going on between Sam and me, and all the things we never got to smooth over, but she doesn't know the half of it.

"And it was so hard seeing you have to go through that," she continues. "Not just her loss, but your guilt about all the things you thought you put her through."

"Things weren't good between us." I don't think I've ever said those words out loud to my sister—only to Jill. It's different speaking to Hilda about this, because she knew Sam well. They were friends. "They hadn't been for a while."

"I know that. As I said, Sam confided in me. More than you think."

I briefly scan Hilda's face. I'm not sure I want her to share with me the things my dead partner told her about me. I also strongly suspect—although, how can I truly be sure?—that Sam wouldn't have told her the details, the crux of it all.

"I went through the change before you did, Hera. I know all about it," Hilda says.

I huff out a nervous chuckle. "You're my sister and I love you dearly, but I'm not sure I want to have this conversation with you."

"We don't have to go into specifics." Hilda leans over the table again. "But it's about time you forgave yourself. Sam's never coming back to tell you that she forgives you for everything. You're the only one who holds that power now."

I shake my head. "I'm not sure I ever can. She died too soon, too suddenly for that. We were meant to get past that bump in our road together and her death meant we couldn't. That we never will." Tears sting behind my eyes. "When she died," my throat swells, "we hadn't spoken in days. Not had a proper conversation, anyway. I hadn't told her I loved her for a very long time. For all I knew, we might not even have made it. If she had lived."

"You were together for a very long time," Hilda says. "Every marriage, every single partnership goes through the lowest of lows. It's human nature. It's life and life will always happen. And death, unfortunately, waits for no one."

"I just wish…" I try to push the tears back where they came from. "I wish I'd had a chance to tell her that, despite everything, I still loved her."

"Hera." Hilda looks me straight in the eye. "Of course she knew."

"I certainly didn't show her."

"You don't always have to show somebody you love them." She narrows her eyes. "Trust me, Sam knew. And I know because she told me. Okay? Because I told her how bloody stubborn you could be sometimes and how you needed time to adjust to certain changes but that all of that didn't mean that you loved her any less."

I can't hold back the tears now as I look at my sister and a thought that I haven't been able to articulate shoots through my mind. A thought I could never share with my sister.

If I couldn't allow Sam, the woman I loved more than anything and anyone—my partner who died on me before I had the chance to figure any of this out for myself—to touch me, how could I ever allow anyone else to do so again?

Chapter Thirty-Five

KAT

When I arrive at Hera's, I have no idea what might happen. Even though she stayed over on Wednesday, her warm, naked body pressed against me throughout the night, nothing else happened and not much more was said.

We've spoken on the phone since, but Hera is a woman who needs to be experienced live. Half of what she wants to say, but can't express with words, I need to read off her face and translate from her body language.

She opens the door wide and kisses me on the cheek, almost politely.

Once she has closed the door, she grins at me, and says, "Please tell me tomorrow's Rocco's turn to open the Pink Bean?"

I nod. "We take turns on Saturdays and I opened last week, so." I look into Hera's eyes and something in her glance tells me this Friday evening will be very different from the last. Not because she will—miraculously—allow me to be all over her tonight, but because she appears to no longer be in the paralyzing grip of fear.

"Good." Only then, does she pull me close. She wraps

her arms around me. "I need to tell you something," she whispers in my ear.

———

It's a beautiful evening and Hera's taken me to her back patio. She has fixed us each a grapefruit mimosa—I've let it slip that it's my favorite tipple.

"I'm not very good at explaining things." She holds up her hands. "I think that's why I was so dead set on becoming a builder. At least in my choice of profession I could express myself with my hands."

You've expressed yourself plenty with your hands already, I want to say, but I know it's not appropriate. She wants to tell me something that is important and difficult. My attention can't help but be sidetracked for a moment by her big strong hands, though.

She sips from her mimosa and pulls a bit of a face. "Did I put too much grapefruit juice in?" she asks.

"No. They're perfect."

"Okay, if you say so."

"I do." I send her an encouraging smile.

"When Sam…" She clears her throat and starts again. "When Sam died we were… How to put this? We were going through somewhat of a cold war period in our relationship. Things were not good. Not in our daily life and certainly not in the bedroom." Hera stares at the liquid in her glass. I can already tell a grapefruit mimosa will never be her drink—for starters, it's way too pink for her.

"It had been going on for a while. It's one of the reasons I sought therapy. Even though, sadly, Jill couldn't fix me quickly enough for Sam and me to make up before she died. For me to take that crucial first step to repair our relationship." She snickers. "In a way, it's kind of silly. But hindsight and all that, you know." She drinks and pulls a face again. "I was going through menopause and it not only seriously fucked with my head, it fucked with my body as well. I tried all sorts of things. Every patch and hormone treatment you can think of, but nothing really seemed to help. I got more sullen, more depressed, ever more disgusted by my body. I grew so unbelievably uncomfortable in my skin, of course I didn't want Sam to touch me. I stopped touching her as well. We stopped having sex altogether. Which didn't help matters." Hera briefly looks me in the eye, then glances away again.

"To cut a long story short. We grew more and more apart. Most nights I slept in the spare room. I didn't know what to do with myself and with this whole menopause and midlife crisis business. It's as though it plunged me into this big existential crisis. Things were bad. And then she died." Hera's voice breaks. "She was just gone."

I wish we didn't have this table between us. I need to stop myself from getting up and throwing my arms around her. But I can tell Hera's not done yet. She has more to say.

"The ironic thing is that after Sam died, my doctor tried me on a new hormone replacement combo that actually worked. I started feeling better about myself." She sighs. "Of course by then she was gone and I no longer had the chance to tell her how stupid I'd been. How disrespectful of her needs and her desires. Disrespectful of our relationship as well because I'd had actual thoughts of leaving her." Hera wraps her fingers tightly around the delicate Champagne flute. "Try standing upright in front of your dead partner's coffin then." In one swift movement, she brings the flute to her lips and knocks back all of its contents. "The truly excruciating part was that it was all in my head. I got trapped in this infinite loop in my mind, because, once she was gone, all I wanted was for her to come back. But I could only see it then, when she was already dead. When it was too late." She puts her glass down and pinches the bridge of her nose.

"Hera," I whisper. "I'm so sorry you had to go through that."

"She was the woman I loved and I hadn't kissed her for weeks. How's that for loving someone?" Hera's voice breaks, but then she seems to regroup. She straightens her frame. She's still staring straight ahead. As though she's still afraid to look at me—as though what she has just told me might make me dislike her, while it only makes me grow fonder of her. Because I know this is hard for her, but she's having the courage to show herself to me. She's finding the words she believed were so unspeakable.

"Hera." I can't stop myself any longer. I get up. I need to touch her. I need to make her feel some warmth. I crouch in front of her and put my hands on her knees. "I'm sure Sam understood, if not all, then at least part of what you were going through. Isn't that what the people we love do? They know us better than we know ourselves and they understand us, through the good and the bad."

"I treated her so appallingly that, after she died, I vowed to never enter into a relationship again. I think the coping mechanism I developed when I was at my worst, the complete shutdown of any physical intimacy, has become so ingrained in my mind that I don't know how to get past it now. Even when my body is clearly telling me it wants more." Hera looks down at me. Her mouth is set in a downward grimace. I just want to kiss it off her. I want to see a smile on her face again as soon as possible. But I can't kiss her yet. I can only make my intentions known by gently squeezing her knee.

"I can understand how awful Sam dying like that must have been for you. She was still so young and you were going through that rough patch, but Hera, you're still alive. You're not dead. You need to find a way to live your life without punishing yourself."

"Turns out that's bloody hard to do." Hera looks me in the eye. Her face has softened although I can still see the struggle in it. The battle between wanting to chastise herself eternally for being what she considers a below-par partner and what meeting me has awakened in her.

"I dare to disagree." I push myself up because this crouch is getting quite uncomfortable. I hold out my hand to her. "It certainly doesn't have to be as hard as you're making it."

She takes my hand but doesn't get up.

"How about, just for tonight, we go about things a little differently?" I may not have a great relationship track record, but I do have some experience in making people let their guard down. "How about…" I give her hand a tug and she lets me pull her up.

"You're surprisingly strong." Hera grins at me as we come face to face. "How about what?"

"How about we go inside and we approach this from the opposite direction?"

"Can you be a bit less cryptic, please?" She grins at me.

"I know you're scared. And I know you have an endless stream of thoughts running through your head. But I also know, for an absolute, indisputable fact, that you want me. Why don't you let me show you just a tiny glimpse of how things can be between us and we take things from there? Who knows, maybe we can silence some of those voices in your head for good." I inch closer to her. "All due respect to Sam, for your loss, and what you went through, but I'm not Sam. I'm Katherine. My more extravagant friends some-times call me K.Jo. And I'm here for you, because, guess what, Hera Walker?" I bring my lips to her ear. "I think I'm falling in love with you."

She lets go of my hands and curls her arms around me, holding me close.

"I think I might be falling in love with you too." Hera mumbles her words, but I hear them loud and clear. They reverberate in my ear for a long time after.

Chapter Thirty-Six

HERA

KAT LEADS me inside my own house. Maybe we should have met at her place, where there aren't so many pictures of Sam strewn across the lounge.

But I let Katherine take the lead. I need to let her. I know what will happen if I take it from her. My brain will start short-circuiting again and I will thwart all her wonderful, thoughtful intentions.

Even though I invited Katherine over to have a much-needed chat, I think I've said all I can say for one night. I've said more than I have said to anyone—apart from Jill—in a very long time.

Last night's conversation with Hilda had me tossing and turning for a while, her words rummaging through my head, keeping me awake, until I found some small comfort in the fact that Sam could, at least, talk to Hilda, while I shut myself off from her. While I was trying to explain something to Jill that I would only truly come to understand after Sam died.

I needed time and I didn't know we wouldn't have the

time. But I realize that I couldn't know this then. It was impossible for me to know that Sam's time was up when I rebuffed her advances for the umpteenth time, saying, "Later." I wasn't to know that, for the two of us, there was no more later.

Hilda was right. I'm the only one who can forgive myself for that. And just maybe, Katherine leading me up the stairs of my own house the way she's doing now, can help me with that. Because one thing's for sure: I need a little help. Frankly, I need all the help I can get. Because I'm still alive, even though, for the longest time, it felt like a crucial part of me had died with Sam.

Kat stops in front of my bedroom door.

"I'm not going to do one single thing you don't want me to do," she says solemnly. "But do know that every single thing I do, I'll want to do with all my heart."

She stands in front of me the way I've come to know her. So tall and charismatic and impossible to ignore. For a split second, it occurs to me how foolish I was to walk away from her last Sunday. A woman like this. The exact same sentiment applied to Sam when I had thoughts about leaving her, while all I ever really wanted was to be with her. Even though I didn't know how to do it, how to break through that wall. I had no clue how to demolish the thought patterns I had carefully constructed to save myself from some upcoming pain—while the most excruciating pain was already tearing me apart. Tearing us apart.

It's for Sam that I nod at Katherine. It's for Sam that, today, I decide to trust Kat and her great big heart—because Hilda was right about that as well. It's for Sam that I'm letting Katherine in. I'll never get the chance to do that with Sam anymore. But Sam is dead and I'm alive. And here I stand, gazing into Kat's dark eyes.

"You're so beautiful," I say. And maybe because of the darkness in my heart I didn't think I deserved to be touched by such beauty. But my mind is changing. Three women who have survived with me have taken care of that. My sister, my therapist, and Katherine Jones. My nephew's best friend. A woman I deemed so incompatible with me, I sabotaged my feelings for her from the very beginning.

"Right back at you," Kat says, and her smile melts me to the very core. "Shall we go in?" she asks, her voice soft and warm.

"Yes, please."

She opens the door and we walk into my bedroom.

Once inside, something about Katherine changes, a slight shift in her demeanor. As though, now that's she's gotten me over the threshold of this room, she knows she's got me.

She might be right.

She brings her hand to the top button of my shirt—I dressed up for her visit—and asks, "May I take this off?" Her head is tilted and her voice husky and low.

I couldn't even protest if I wanted to. Something in me has changed as well.

"You don't have to ask permission for everything you do," I say. "I trust you, and you need to trust me to let you know when I want you to stop."

"Deal." Katherine's smile is so wide and inviting that, before she has the chance to undo one of my buttons, I pull her in for a kiss.

This kiss is different from all the others we have exchanged since we met, because, as I kiss her, I let go of my biggest fear. Whenever a thought creeps up on me that I'm betraying Sam or myself or, even, deceiving Katherine by doing this, by allowing this, I shut it down firmly. I talk back, the way Jill has taught me to do, something I never seemed to have gotten the hang of until now—and I simply enjoy the exquisite sensation of Katherine's lips on mine.

I enjoy the anticipation, the thrill in the air, because I'm no longer afraid of what might happen. I'm no longer wasting all my energy and focus on coming up with plausible excuses for why I want her to stop. The biggest excuse dissolving when I told her the truth. When I admitted my inadequacies as a partner and a lover. Not only to her, but to myself. I've not forgiven myself for any of that just yet. But Katherine has promised to help me with that and, just as I trust her to only have my very best interests at heart when she removes my jeans later—as I know she will—I trust that she will help me with finding that forgiveness somewhere inside myself as well.

She has already done so much for me.

"You're distracting me from the task at hand," she says, when we break from our kiss. Her red lipstick is smeared all over her mouth and the sight of it makes me smile. It's a smile that emanates all the way from my core. My entire body is smiling as I look at Katherine, as I take her in, drink her in, let her presence overwhelm me. As I relinquish control in a way I haven't been able to do in years. Sometimes you need to start over, I think, as my gaze follows the motions of Kat's hands on my buttons. Sometimes you need to hit that reset button and try again. Because being with Katherine will never erase who I was with Sam, on my good days and my bad days, but it will give me a chance to try to be my best self again.

She guides my shirt off and ogles my bra. But before she touches me again, she hoists her own top over her head and gets rid of her own bra first.

The sight of her bare breasts makes my mouth water. I've

been such a fool to deny myself this because standing here with Kat, knowing, in every fiber of my being what's going to happen next, makes me feel much more alive than I ever was in the months before Sam died. It's a hard thing to admit but it's also a comforting thought, because this is how life is. It knocks you down one day, only to pick you up the next.

Sometimes I'm happy, sometimes I'm sad; mostly, I'm somewhere in between. Then a woman like Katherine comes along, a woman with her own myriad of complications, but a woman so radiant, so confident, so sure of herself when she comes for me, it would be foolish to resist any further. It would be foolish to resist that burst of happiness she brings with her when she walks through my door. When, as now, she brings her hands to my back, and unhooks my bra.

She throws it onto a chair, then looks me in the eye, before dropping her gaze. Her glance on my breasts makes my nipples rise up, as though they're reaching toward her. She glances up at me again, briefly, looking for signs of me wanting her to stop—but I don't want her to stop.

She lifts her hands to my breasts and cups them ever so gently. Her touch is so warm, so exhilarating, such a shocking reminder of things I'd never thought I'd feel again, a single tear rolls down my cheek. It falls off my chin, onto the back of her hand. She leans in and kisses it away, while her hands softly cup my breasts.

It's then I know that someone like Katherine is what I've needed all along. Someone to kiss away my tears, to break down my walls, to give me pleasure once again. As her fingers curl around my nipples, I'm beginning to believe that I might just deserve it—that I might just deserve her.

I revel in the sensation of her hands on my breasts, her fingers on my nipples. I keep my eyes wide open so I can see her face. A small part of me is afraid that, when I close them,

I'll see Sam's face. With that look she gave me toward the end. All desperation and need. So I focus on Katherine's lovely features. Her big brown eyes. The lipstick I smudged on her lips earlier. She tilts her head a little. Another question. But it's one I don't have to reply to, not anymore. She can read it in my eyes now, I'm sure of that.

Kat lifts my breast to her lips and takes my nipple in her mouth. I do close my eyes then—her face is out of view anyway. On the back of my eyelids, while Kat's tongue skates along my nipple, I don't see Sam. I don't see anything at all. And isn't that the point of closing my eyes? To no longer see and to magnify the sensation of her tongue lavishing itself on my nipple. Because that's what it feels like. She started off gently, but now she's sucking my nipple into her mouth and all I feel is her hunger for me. The difference with the last time I faced Kat's hunger is that, now, I feed off of it myself. My desire grows with hers. My thoughts are no longer in the way. Kat wants me and I want her. It really can be that simple.

Before Kat focuses on my other nipple, she pauses briefly. I open my eyes and catch her glancing up at me. God, her eyes. In them I see a blend of kindness and unbridled lust. It's not the first time I've come across that look in her eyes. It's the kind of look, I know now, that will thaw the coldest of ice queens. How did I manage to resist it before? Because I sure can't do that anymore now.

I give her a slight nod of the head so she'll know I want more. Much more.

Instead of enveloping my other nipple with her lips, she takes my hand and leads me to the bed. We lie down, I on my back and Kat half on top of me. Our breasts are pressed together and I don't know what I want more. For Kat to lick my nipples again or for her to gaze into my eyes like this for a good while longer.

"I want you," I say. My voice is not shy or timid—there's not a glimmer of doubt in it. I want it all. I want her.

"You've got me," she says, and kisses me on the lips, while her hand meanders to the button of my jeans.

My limbs don't stiffen—nothing about me is rigid anymore. My body welcomes her because my mind's letting her in.

As she lowers my zipper, it's as though, with that act, she lowers the last barrier around my heart—around my desire. It's a freeing action, one that makes me tug my jeans off my legs in an almost helpless manner. But Kat is here to calm me down. She doesn't say anything, she just puts her hand on my belly, which falls and rises quickly in time with my sharp, intoxicated intakes of breath.

Then I realize I was wrong. Taking off my jeans wasn't the final barrier. Spreading my legs for her is. There's so much release in the simple motion of letting my knees fall apart. It's an invitation. A heartfelt invitation for her to enter my most intimate space. It's where I want her. But first, there's that look again. I can still make out some kindness in her eyes, but they're so dark with desire now that her glance raking over my body is enough for me to respond. And respond I do. By lowering my underwear. By freeing the path for her. And sure, she has seen me naked before, but this is a totally different kind of nakedness. This is me opening up to her, as wide as I will ever go. This is me under the spell of desire, under the spell of Katherine Jones.

Kat takes over and, torturously slow, guides the last piece of clothing off me. I need to spread for her—again. The flow of air between my legs is thrilling. My clit stands to immediate attention, which baffles me most of all. The way my body has taken over, whereas before, it was my mind that was in full control.

I'm not sure how she's done it, but in a matter of

seconds, Kat is naked as well. She must have picked up some special skills in her former life. I amaze myself again by being able to think of her like that, like the escort that she used to be, and not shut down completely. On the contrary. I open up more, spread my legs a little wider for her.

"I want you," I repeat, nothing but urgency in my tone now. All the years without this blissful kind of intimacy catch up with me in that moment, a moment that's been building since I met Kat.

She doesn't respond with words this time but, instead, nestles herself between my legs. She kisses my lower belly while her hands reach for my breasts. Involuntarily, at least that's how it seems, my hips move toward her. I feel her nipples against my thighs but, most of all, I feel her body close to my clit. Close, but still too far.

Kat kisses a path down my belly to my inner thighs. She peppers me with hot, wet kisses—all promises of what's to come.

I bury my hands in her hair because I need to hold on to something—to her. Her lips are inches away from my clit. I can feel her breath on me there already. Years of sensual deprivation pool in my core. All my lust focused on one woman and what she's doing to me with her mouth. Her lips are just above my clit now, and already, I'm close to exploding. To reaching the ultimate surrender. Because I was wrong once again. *This* is the final stage. The moment her tongue connects with my clit.

Her mouth on me there is unspeakably warm. It sparks in me such a rush of lightness, I may as well be levitating off the bed. I feel like I've just taken the most potent happiness drug on the planet—maybe I have.

Kat licks me between my legs and I feel it everywhere, in every last fiber of my being. It changes the fabric of me forever. I already know that, after this, I won't be the same.

Every time she flicks her tongue over my clit, I'm a fraction further removed from the bitter, buttoned-up woman I allowed myself to become. And I know, deep in my heart, that this was the only way for me to break out of this shell.

At last, I'm ready.

Acknowledgments

When I first conceived of the idea for the Pink Bean series, it was never going to consist of more than nine books. From the very beginning, I had Book 9 planned as a big farewell to the series. But, as so often happens in a writer's life, the characters disagreed with me.

To be clear: this is NOT the final book in the series. I already know who Pink Bean 10 will be about (there are some hints in what you've just read—do email me with your guesses!) and, currently, I have plans to go up to twelve books in the series. This might very well change again, even though I will focus more on other series and books in 2019.

All this to say that I keep on enjoying writing this series enormously. It has given me so much and I love returning to it. Your kind words about it have also made a big difference to me. I'd like to thank each and every one of you who has left a review on one of my books and/or has emailed me about them. I'm not always quick to reply, but I appreciate it so very much.

As always, I owe huge gratitude to my not-so-secret weapon: my wife (who keeps putting the writing of her very own book on hold because she's such a huge part of my writerly process.) I honestly couldn't do any of this without Caroline.

For years now I've had the privilege to call Cheyenne Blue my editor and, more importantly, my friend. These days, when I revise, I always have a voice in the back of my head asking: what will Cheyenne have to say about this? Undoubtedly, this mild form of lesfic writer merging makes me a better writer.

A huge thank-you also to my lovely beta-reader Carrie and my super-efficient proofreader Claire. Side note: I've started calling Caroline, Cheyenne, Carrie and Claire 'The Four C's Who Make Everything Better'!

The members of my Launch Team continue to be all kinds of amazing: from typo spotting to much-needed enthusiastic reactions when I first unleash a book onto the world (always a delicate time in a writer's life), their support means the world to me.

And, of course, thank you, Dear Reader, for making it to Book 9. Here's to at least three more!

Thank you.

About the Author

Harper Bliss is the author of the *Pink Bean* series, the *High Rise* series, the *French Kissing* serial and many other lesbian romance titles. She is the co-founder of Ladylit Publishing and My LesFic weekly newsletter.

Harper loves hearing from readers and you can get in touch with her here:

www.harperbliss.com
harperbliss@gmail.com

Printed in Poland
by Amazon Fulfillment
Poland Sp. z o.o., Wrocław

53861718R00127